OUTNUMBERED...

"They's no place for you to run, mister, so whyn't you give it up. We won't hurt you none. Just take that fine-lookin' horse and the mule. Take them an' whatever else you got." He laughed. "But we won't touch a hair on your old gray head."

Joe frowned. "Am I really starting to get some gray in my hair?"

"Damn you, mister, you ain't takin' us serious."

"Why should I worry about a bunch of dead men?"

Howard turned to his brothers and shouted, "Get him, boys. Cut him good."

Thomas started circling around Joe in one direction, Benjamin in the other. Joe suspected that their plan—one they must have used before with a successful outcome—was for the three of them to trap him in the center of a triangle so that his back had to be toward at least one of them at all times.

It was a perfectly good plan, he conceded. If he allowed them to carry it out . . .

BLOOD
AT BEAR LAKE

A Man of Honor Novel

GARY FRANKLIN

B
BERKLEY BOOKS, NEW YORK

THE BERKLEY PUBLISHING GROUP
Published by the Penguin Group
Penguin Group (USA) Inc.
375 Hudson Street, New York, New York 10014, USA
Penguin Group (Canada), 90 Eglinton Avenue East, Suite 700, Toronto, Ontario M4P 2Y3, Canada
(a division of Pearson Penguin Canada Inc.)
Penguin Books Ltd., 80 Strand, London WC2R 0RL, England
Penguin Group Ireland, 25 St. Stephen's Green, Dublin 2, Ireland (a division of Penguin Books Ltd.)
Penguin Group (Australia), 250 Camberwell Road, Camberwell, Victoria 3124, Australia
(a division of Pearson Australia Group Pty. Ltd.)
Penguin Books India Pvt. Ltd., 11 Community Centre, Panchsheel Park, New Delhi—110 017, India
Penguin Group (NZ), 67 Apollo Drive, Rosedale, North Shore 0632, New Zealand
(a division of Pearson New Zealand Ltd.)
Penguin Books (South Africa) (Pty.) Ltd., 24 Sturdee Avenue, Rosebank, Johannesburg 2196,
South Africa

Penguin Books Ltd., Registered Offices: 80 Strand, London WC2R 0RL, England

This is a work of fiction. Names, characters, places, and incidents either are the product of the author's imagination or are used fictitiously, and any resemblance to actual persons, living or dead, business establishments, events, or locales is entirely coincidental.

BLOOD AT BEAR LAKE

A Berkley Book / published by arrangement with the author

PRINTING HISTORY
Berkley edition / August 2008

ISBN: 978-0-425-22292-8

BERKLEY®
Berkley Books are published by The Berkley Publishing Group,
a division of Penguin Group (USA) Inc.,
375 Hudson Street, New York, New York 10014.
BERKLEY is a registered trademark of Penguin Group (USA) Inc.
The "B" design is a trademark belonging to Penguin Group (USA) Inc.

PRINTED IN THE UNITED STATES OF AMERICA

10 9 8 7 6 5 4 3 2 1

✢ 1 ✢

A MAN WILL NOT keep his scalp very long in the mountains if he lacks patience. Patience was a trait Joe Moss learned as a young free trapper in the Rockies, and he still had it as a man in his early forties. He also still had his own scalp, no thanks to some.

Trapper, trader, freighter, miner, and sometimes fugitive, Moss had led a rough-and-tumble life and bore the scars to prove it. On the other hand, he had inflicted far more scars than ever he'd received. And he had taken a great many scalps over the years.

Now, newly married, with a wife whose whereabouts he did not know and with a daughter who was denied to him, Moss found himself in a tight spot. Literally.

In ducking away from a mob of hired assassins, he had plunged into what might well prove to be an inescapable trap.

After years of searching, Joe had finally reunited with

the love of his life, Fiona McCarthy. In his absence, she had borne him a child, but while they were apart, Fiona was accused of murder. To protect her, she gave their four-year-old daughter, Jessica, to an order of nuns at St. Mary of the Mountain church in Carson City, Nevada.

Joe was with Fiona barely long enough to be legally married to her—an event they had not quite gotten around to before they were separated five years earlier—and to make an appearance outside the convent to reclaim their daughter. Fiona, and now Joe as well, were hated by the wealthy and powerful Peabody brothers, who wholly owned one of the top-producing mines on the Comstock Lode.

When Joe and Fiona reached the gates of the convent, they were immediately attacked by a paid mob of the Peabody thugs. Joe held the attackers off to give Fiona time to escape, but he was surrounded and greatly outnumbered.

Father O'Connor, the priest who oversaw both the church and the convent, offered Joe sanctuary, but the priest and Joe knew better than to think the mob would honor the age-old sanctuary of the altar. O'Connor shoved Joe into a tiny space carved out of solid rock, the entrance to which was concealed by a bookcase in the priest's private office.

Now Joe was trapped there, with a howling mob searching for him throughout the church and its outbuildings. Joe had only his Colt revolving pistol, his bowie knife, and his ever-present and fearsome tomahawk to defend himself.

He might as well have been weaponless. If he was discovered, neither bullets nor steel would be enough to extricate him from this trap.

Which suggested he damned well better *not* allow himself to be caught.

Joe checked his weapons, then silently investigated the limits of the artificial cave where he was trapped.

In pitch-dark, he felt his way to the back. Cold, slightly

jagged stone was all his seeking hands encountered. The hole ran less than two paces deep, and was not quite high enough for Joe's six-foot-plus height to come fully upright. He could touch both side walls at the same time simply by extending his arms. The floor was uneven and littered with stone chips.

Joe had no idea why such a hole might have been carved from the rock. Perhaps it was to have been the start of a mine adit that was abandoned when no ore was discovered. Perhaps it was intended as a concealed storage place for church purposes that he could not imagine.

Whatever the reason, it would make a most uncomfortable coffin.

Joe had to get the hell out of there. Every moment he spent in there, Fiona was getting farther and farther away from him.

The last he saw of her was a tiny moving figure and a stream of dust raised by the hooves of her madly racing sorrel mare as she ran to escape her tormentors.

And, dammit, he did not know where she was bound.

He would follow her to the ends of the earth or to the end of his days, whichever came first.

But that would be after he got out of this miserable damned hole in the ground.

Joe sat gingerly, sweeping loose rock from under his butt, careful to make no noise while he did so. He leaned back against the stone wall and closed his eyes, willing his muscles to rest but concentrating his entire being on the faint sounds that came from the other side of that bookcase.

". . . that sonuvabitch . . . we'll find . . . we do you'll pay, Priest . . . then we . . ."

The voice was not one Joe had heard before and he could not hear it clearly, but it was a voice he intended to remember. Perhaps it belonged to the last living Peabody

3

brother—Joe had already killed the other two—but perhaps not.

Had he been sure it was Peabody himself who was speaking, Joe would have stepped out and killed the son of a bitch, inside a church or not. Killing the last Peabody might well be enough to call off the dogs who were after Fiona for a murder he was sure his gentle wife could never have committed, no matter what the Peabodys claimed.

But there were simply too many in the mob whose voices and boots he could hear out there. He could not kill them all, although he would have been glad to if that gave Fiona freedom from fear. Even if it meant his own death, Joe would gladly have leaped into the fray if he only was assured that Fiona would be free.

All he could do, dammit, was to sit there, slumped against the cold, gritty stone, and wait. And wait.

✦ 2 ✦

JOE WOKE WITH a start, aware that he had dropped off
to sleep but with no notion of how long he had been sleeping. He was sure of one thing, though. It was long enough to
fill his bladder. He had to take a piss that would float a boat.

Outside his hole in the rock, beyond the bookcase that
concealed this spot, he could hear voices. Louder now than
they had been and, he thought, closer.

"You're gonna tell us, you old son of a bitch," someone
snarled. "The boss wants t' know and you're either gonna
tell us where he is or I'll cut your useless balls off."

There was a muffled sound that might have been a slap,
and then another.

"Tell us, damn you."

Joe could hear mumbling. It was in the cadence of a
prayer.

"Hold the old bastard still, Charlie, while I slice one o'
his ears off'n his head," the voice said.

5

There was a sound of scuffling and some more slaps, then a sharp cry.

"What? You don't think I'll do it, old man? You think your papist ways are gonna help you now? Dammit, Charlie, hold 'im still so's I can get a clean cut. I wouldn't want t' ruin his looks with a ragged cut, now would I? Them nuns wouldn't let him fuck 'em if I went an' made him ugly."

Joe could hear laughter.

He could also hear his own blood coursing hot through his veins.

Gunfire would draw attention back here, but steel is silent. And just as deadly.

With the remembered cadence of a Lakota war chant going through his mind, Joe slipped his bowie from its sheath and held it loosely in his left hand. In his right was his deadly tomahawk.

He was not sure how many armed men were in the priest's office with Father O'Connor. At least two. But why worry about details?

He rose into a crouch, finished the Lakota prayer, and pushed the bookcase open.

The heavy set of shelving moved ponderously forward, squealing a little as seldom-used hinges grated metal on metal.

"What the—?"

The thug who stood over Father O'Connor never had time to finish his sentence. Joe took two long steps forward, and his wicked tomahawk split the man's skull wide open. He went down, spilling blood and brains onto the stone floor.

There were two others in the small room. They clawed for their pistols.

Joe quickly retrieved his tomahawk and threw it at the one who was standing off to the side of the room. The 'hawk spun end over end and landed blade-first in the middle of the fellow's breastbone. The man looked down at the 'hawk protruding from his chest. He went pale and began to sag to his knees, no longer interested in his or anyone else's firearms.

The man who had been holding Father O'Connor's arms behind him blanched and tried to use the priest as a human shield.

Joe was able, if just barely, to suppress an impulse to shout a triumphant war cry as he leaped the short distance between him and Father O'Connor's assailant. Joe's bowie flashed and the man fell back, his throat open and blood spurting half-a-dozen feet across the room.

"Bastards!"

Joe retrieved his tomahawk and returned it to his sash, then quickly began relieving the dead men of their scalps. One of them had red hair. His scalp would make a fine addition to Joe's collection. It needed replenishment badly after his friend, the widow Ellen Johnson, had discarded all of his old scalps some months earlier.

"No. You can't . . . you mustn't do that!" O'Connor protested.

"Hell, there ain't no harm of it."

"No, really, I can't allow it. This is sacred ground."

"T' you maybe. Wasn't to them. An' if the truth be known, it ain't sacred to me neither." Joe ripped the scalp from the head of the first man he had killed there.

The priest looked like he was going to be sick. The man stood there with his clerical robes in disarray, his spindly legs on display. He seemed not to notice that, however. "Stop this, Moss, or I will never consent to let Jessica go back to her mother."

Joe grunted and finished scalping the second man, then moved to the last, the one who had caught the tomahawk in his chest. He was still alive, although barely. Joe picked his head up and began cutting.

"Do you hear me, Moss? You will never so much as see that little girl again."

"You promised t' return her to her mother. You gave your word. You never gave me nothing but grief, Priest. Now quit your prattling an' tell me how I can get out o' here. Are there others of Peabody's men out there?"

O'Connor nodded. "Yes. I think so, yes."

"How many?"

"I don't know that. A dozen. Possibly more."

"Do you know where they're waiting?"

"No, I do not."

"Would you tell me if you did?"

Father O'Connor drew himself to his full height and with dignity said, "I would not bring harm down upon you, Joe Moss, any more than I would bring harm to your wife. Or to your daughter either, for that matter. I will pray for the deliverance of your soul. If I could do anything to help deliver your body from evil, I would do that, too."

Joe looked the priest up and down, thinking. Then he grunted. "You got any more of those robe things, Padre?"

"My cassock, you mean? Yes, why do you ask?"

"'Cause I want to borrow one. And one o' those funny-looking hats you guys wear."

"I have a biretta, of course, but I only use it . . ."

"Where is it?" Joe interrupted. "I'm in a bit of a hurry here, Padre. If you don't mind."

"My cassock and biretta are in that wardrobe over there, but I cannot allow . . ."

"Thanks." Joe snatched the wardrobe door open and pulled out the cassock. He slipped it on over his clothing and stuffed his Stetson hat beneath the voluminous robe, then perched the biretta on top of his head.

Blood at Bear Lake

Already six feet two, with black hair and weathered flesh, with the biretta he probably looked as big as a grizzly. But as harmless as a kitten.

He hoped.

"Is there a side door, Padre?"

The priest pointed. "There is a covered corridor that leads to the convent, but you are not permitted to . . ." By then he was speaking to an empty room. Joe Moss was already on his way out of Father O'Connor's office and headed toward the convent. The convent where Jessica was.

✦ 3 ✦

T HE FIRST THING Joe did when he reached the corridor that connected the church to the convent was to open the priest's robes and take a leak into the bushes that were struggling to survive in this stony, arid soil.

While he stood there watering the plants, he could see one pair of armed men standing guard at the front of the church. Another two patrolled back and forth along the road that ran past it.

He had slept longer than he realized when he was in that hole in the ground. It was well past sundown now. Joe welcomed the shadows. They would help him get away without endangering the nuns or—more important—little Jessica.

But if he could see her, even speak to her before he left . . .

Joe scowled. He did not dare try to push his luck that far. If Peabody's men discovered his attachment to the child, they could well take her hostage. He would not put it past them, and the last thing in the world Joe would ever do would be to place his daughter in harm's way.

He had no more than gotten a glimpse of her, but already he loved her more than life itself, and as soon as he could find Fiona they would take Jessica back and be a family.

As soon as he could find Fiona.

Joe's scowl deepened and turned into a sigh. He rearranged the robes and hurried along the corridor, letting himself into the convent at the other end.

"Father, I . . . who are you? I haven't seen you here before. Are you passing through? Is there anything you need?" The nun looked mildly confused but not alarmed. "Is Father O'Connor with you? Is he all right?" She shuddered. "There was shooting earlier today. Very close to the church, it was."

Joe wanted to tell her to shut the hell up, but that was probably not the best idea. He let her prattle on for a moment, then asked, "Do you have a horse I can use?"

"We? A horse? No, of course not. Whatever use would we have for a horse?"

"No, of course not. I tell you what, Sister, whyn't you guide me over to the other side of this place."

She gave him a questioning look, but did not voice her reaction to what must have seemed a very odd request. "Of course, Father."

Father. No one had ever called Joe "Father" before. Under the circumstances, with Jessica somewhere within these walls, it seemed strange to him. And kind of nice, too. "Thank you."

"Will you be hearing confessions, Father? Or assisting Father O'Connor with Mass?"

Joe ignored her, and after a minute or so it got through

to the nun that he was not feeling chatty. She hushed up and led the way.

He followed as the nun silently led him through a maze of handsomely appointed rooms to the far side of the convent. Joe kept looking anxiously to either side, hoping he might see Jessica, but the only thing he saw were a few black-robed nuns going about the humdrum chores of institutional living.

The convent was dimly lighted—thank goodness—and eerily silent. Not that he minded that. Silent beat the hell out of the fusillade of gunfire that would erupt if he were seen and recognized.

"This is the other side, the side toward Virginia City," the nun said, stopping abruptly when they reached a long hallway that was lined with a series of small rooms on one side and corresponding small stained-glass windows on the other. "Is the diocese planning an expansion, Father? Is that why you are here?"

Instead of answering, Joe asked, "Do those windows open?"

"Oh, I shouldn't think so. We've never had any reason to open them. We get quite enough fresh air without that." She tilted her head. "Why would you ask a thing like that?"

"'Cause I'm gonna open one of them," Joe said.

"Why would you . . . ?"

Joe ignored her. He stepped closer and took a look at the window frame. It was permanently fixed in place and not intended to be opened.

What the hell!

He removed his biretta and handed it to the puzzled nun, then shrugged out of the cassock, too, and let it fall off his shoulders and slide to the stone floor.

Joe put his Stetson back onto his head and winked. "Thanks, Sister. I owe you one."

Blood at Bear Lake

He pulled his Colt's revolving pistol from his holster—he thought the nun was going to faint dead away when he did so—and used the butt to carefully break the nearest stained-glass window.

Then he proceeded to climb through the vacant window frame and lower himself to the ground outside while the nun watched in stunned silence the behavior of this very strange new priest.

✛ **4** ✛

D AMN NUNS SHOULD have put some effort into land-
scaping, Joe silently grumbled when he hit the ground
outside the convent, because he sure could have used some
bushes to get behind. Crouched there against the bare stone
of the convent walls, he felt like there must have been a
thousand eyes pointing in his direction.

A glance toward the road where Peabody's gunmen
were patrolling back and forth showed that at least at this
moment the coast was clear. Joe turned and went in the opposite direction, staying in his crouch, revolver in one hand
and tomahawk in the other.

If anyone tried to stop him, he would use the tomahawk
if he could, the revolver if he had to.

But he would much prefer to make this getaway in silence and without bloodletting. Since he could not kill
them all, that is. Had he been able to lay waste to Peabody
and every one of his men, Joe would gladly have done that

in order to protect Fiona and little Jessica. Short of that, however, what he wanted right now was to get the hell away from there and find Fiona.

He needed her if he hoped ever to set things right. At this point, he did not even know how it was that Chester Peabody, the eldest of the brothers, came to wind up dead in Fiona's home with a butcher knife in his back. In the magic of reuniting and quickly marrying, Joe had not had a chance to talk with Fiona about that. Did she kill Peabody? If she did, what reason or reasons did she have?

Joe had no idea what her answers to those questions would be, and in truth he really did not much care. What he knew was that he still loved her. Deeply. And Fiona was now his wife in name as well as in deed. Whatever she did or did not do in the past, he would stand with her against all care or torment.

Anything that threatened her, threatened him as well, and he would fight tooth and claw to protect her. And Jessica. Lordy, what a beautiful child Jessica was. It melted his heart just to think about her. Just knowing that Jessica existed made him want to be a better man, made him want to be worthy of the child when finally he and Fiona could reclaim her from the convent and become a family.

All of that, though, would depend on him first getting away from Peabody's men so he could follow Fiona, find her, and somehow return to recover Jessica from Father O'Connor and the nuns.

Joe ran swift and silent through the night. His Henry rifle was lost, somewhere behind where he had dropped it once it ran empty. The Henry repeater would make a fine trophy for whichever of Peabody's men found it, but no matter. He could buy another. The important thing was to keep his scalp. And equally important to him was that he find Fiona.

The Palouse horse was gone, too. He had abandoned it outside the church when he had to cover Fiona's escape on her leggy sorrel mare. He hoped, though, that once loose, the Palouse might have drifted back to the last "home" it had known, to the barn behind Beth Hamilton's mansion.

The house there had been destroyed, burned to the ground by the Peabodys, but the barn and tack shed had been intact when Joe and Fiona went there that morning.

Joe stood upright and extended his stride, muttering under his breath the cadences of a Crow war chant.

Because he was indeed intent upon a long and bloody war with those Peabody sons of bitches who threatened his wife and his daughter.

Joe knew exactly the order of things that he intended. First, find Fiona. Second, kill Peabody and any of his men who stood with the son of a bitch. Finally, reclaim Jessica from the nunnery.

But first he needed to get away from Virginia City and find Fiona.

Wherever she had run to, however far, he would follow and he would find her. He *would*!

THE PALOUSE WAS there, standing outside the pen that served as a corral behind the ruins of the Hamilton mansion. Beth's tall gelding was inside the enclosure along with a horse Joe did not recognize. The Palouse had a broken rein, but seemed unharmed.

Joe stripped his bridle off, but left the horse where it was while he crawled inside the pen. "Easy, boys. You know me. Easy now," he said in a soft, soothing voice.

Beth's gelding nickered at the scent of this man with whom it was already familiar. The other horse turned its butt toward him and stamped its forefeet a few times, but did not offer to kick.

Joe opened the shed and tossed a little hay down to keep Beth's horses occupied, then carried an armload to the fence and dumped it outside where the Palouse could reach it. He went back inside and felt along the east wall until he encountered a bridle hanging there. The Palouse

17

was accustomed to its own bit, so Joe took the time to remove a rein and secure it to his bridle instead of taking the whole outfit. Then he returned the bridle to the peg where it had been hanging—that would undoubtedly cause some puzzlement the next time these horses were used—and went for the Palouse.

"Good boy," he mumbled as he slipped the bridle back in place, the Palouse opening its teeth to the bit after only a momentary balk. "Good boy."

That done, he took a moment to ponder.

He knew which direction Fiona took when she fled from Peabody's men. Come daybreak, he would be able to track her from there. With any kind of luck, she would be hiding not too many miles distant.

Joe figured he should be able to find her given a few hours—half a day tops—and then they could begin the second phase of his plan to get Jessica back.

Why, with any luck at all, they could simply slip out from under Peabody's men. Get away from them and sneak back to the church to have that talk with Father O'Connor.

The man had promised Fiona he would return Jessica to her when things worked out to permit that. Having two loving parents who wanted her and were fully prepared to care for her should certainly count toward that delightful end.

They would present themselves to the priest, then take Jessica and be on their way.

Once they were away from Virginia City, Joe would take them where no Peabody gunman would ever find them.

They had money. Joe still had a thousand dollars in his war bag, and he had given Fiona three times that amount. With four thousand dollars, they could buy trade goods and passage upriver on a Missouri River steamer.

Joe knew several different places where a man could build a trading post. He could trade with the Blackfoot and the Lakota. Perhaps some Northern Cheyenne and Crow would come that far north as well, especially if they knew that Man Killer was giving fair prices for good fur.

Those tribes knew him. More to the point, they respected him. They knew Man Killer's words were good. They would come to him with their furs and their hides.

In winter, he might even get in a little trapping of his own.

Not that there was much money in fur these days. But if he had Fiona, well, that was what was important.

They would be safe on the Upper Missouri. They would have a good life there, the three of them. Jessica would have Indian children to play with. Fiona could be her teacher. Joe's, too, for that matter. He had only recently learned to read, and now he had a thirst for it. Fiona could teach him the words he did not yet know.

A smile flickered across his lips as he thought of himself stuffed into a tiny school desk with little Jessica beside him, both learning out of the same primer.

Joe sighed. But that would be then. This was now. And now there were still men out there in the night who sought to kill him and—far worse—to kill his beloved Fiona.

He gathered his reins and slipped lightly into the saddle. It was time to get the hell away from Virginia City so he could get on with his search for Fiona.

✛ **6** ✛

FIONA HAD BEEN headed a little south of east when she scampered away from the trap Peabody had set for her and Joe, but that meant nothing. She surely would know better than to continue in a straight line when there would be men chasing after her who wanted to kill her.

She would have turned toward . . . where? However many points there were on a compass, that was how many directions she could have gone. Well, except for back there to Virginia City. Joe was sure she would know better than to attempt to hide there where every man could inform on her or any man could decide to collect a bounty on her pretty head.

The only other place Joe knew Fiona was familiar with, and comfortable in, was Lake's Crossing, where Joe had found her after their years of separation. And where they had been at long last married.

At the time, Fiona had been staying with friends, a photographer and his wife.

It was not impossible, Joe thought, that she might return there to wait for him.

Joe pointed the Palouse toward Lake's Crossing and hoped for the best. Wherever Fiona had gone, he was only a day behind her. Surely, he would catch up with her soon. They could wait a little while. Perhaps even enlist the help of some other priest or nun to help them get Jessica back from the convent.

And then, then they could start their lives anew. In Wyoming perhaps. There never was country more big or open or empty than beautiful Wyoming. Or in Montana Territory. There were gold strikes in Montana, they said. That meant miners to feed, and Joe knew valleys there where the grass grew belly-deep to a tall horse and where beef would swell up with fat quick as a jackrabbit mated.

That was the ticket. Build a little trading post where he could do some business with whatever Indians were nearby and raise some beef, too. Fresh meat would be worth a fortune in a mining camp.

It would be a good life, he figured, with Fiona and Jessica at his side. He could not ask for anything more.

The Palouse carried him into Lake's Crossing shortly after the break of day. The horse was about used up. Its muscles quivered with fatigue and its walk was a stumbling shamble.

"You done good, boy," Joe said as he slipped to the ground and walked the horse the last half mile. He tied it to the gate in front of the photographer's house and started up the walk, only to realize that the door was closed and the windows shuttered. He walked around back and found the same thing all around. The house appeared to be empty, perhaps even deserted.

Gary Franklin

A woman in the adjacent yard was hanging clothes on a line to dry. Joe removed his hat when he approached her. "Excuse me, ma'am," Joe said. "I'm looking for the man as lives next door there."

She gave Joe a suspicious look. "What do you want with him? Are you a friend of his?"

"Not exactly, ma'am, but my new wife is. Her and me was married in Faxon's house a few days back. She had been stayin' with him and . . ."

"You are Fiona's husband? You are Mr. Moss?"

"Yes'm, that's me."

The lady smiled. "To hear Fiona tell it, you are seven feet tall and handsomer than any other man ever to walk this earth. I see now that she stretched the truth." She laughed. "But only a little. Where is Fiona, by the way? Is she here? Tell her I have some of that dried apple pie that she dotes on. It's fresh." The lady craned her neck and came onto tiptoes, looking toward the street where she obviously expected to see Fiona.

"That's what I was hoping you could tell me, ma'am," Joe said. "I mean about where Fiona is right now. It's a long story, but her and me got separated, and I don't rightly know which way she went from Virginia City."

"You two were fighting already?"

"Not with each other, no, ma'am. I don't figure that will ever happen. But there's some men that want t' harm her. She had to run while I stayed back t' hold them off her. Like I said, we was separated. Now I'm wanting t' find her."

"And the little girl?"

Joe smiled. "We seen her. Just for a minute but . . . we seen her. After I find Fiona again, we'll take her back from them nuns and have a proper life together as a family. That's my plan anyhow. But first I got to find Fiona."

"I wish I could help you, Mr. Moss, but I've not seen her since the two of you left after your wedding."

"An' Faxon? What about him?" Joe asked.

"Oh, he won't be back here for several months, I shouldn't think. He has been communicating with a publisher in New York City. He and his wife have taken a portfolio of his work there to discuss having the the pictures collected in a book. I don't know how long a thing like that takes, but they closed the house and asked me to keep an eye on it until they get back."

"And you haven't seen Fiona this morning?"

"I'm sorry. No."

Joe sighed. "Thanks. Thank you, ma'am. If you see Fiona . . ." He did not know what he should tell the woman to do if Fiona should come here and find the house boarded up and the family gone.

"If she comes here, Mr. Moss, she can stay with me while she waits. I have room enough for her . . . for the little girl, too, if it comes to that . . . and her company would be a pleasure."

"You're mighty kind, ma'am. Thank you."

Joe turned away and walked back to the front of the house.

His impulse was to press on. Never mind that he had no idea where to look next. Wherever it was, he was in a hurry to get there.

He had no choice about it, though. He would have to stay here at least long enough for the Palouse to recoup some strength. The horse needed feed and water and a rest before they could move along.

And Joe had some shopping to do. He still had his Colt revolving pistol and of course his ever-present tomahawk and bowie knife, but he had lost his rifle in the shoot-out back in Virginia City. He felt naked without a rifle and wanted to replace his Henry, preferably with a repeater if he could find one for sale here in Nevada. Men in towns tended to carry short arms or knives but not rifles, so it remained to be seen what sort of long gun he could find.

It couldn't hurt for him to catch a little sleep, too, while the Palouse rested.

But Fiona. Oh, Fiona! Where are you?

✛ 7 ✛

"Two BITS," THE man said. "That includes all the hay he can eat and all the water he can hold, but if you want me to give him grain, that'll be extra."

"How much extra?"

"Ten cents."

"Good grain?"

"Oats. No corn in it but the oats are clean. There's no mold in them nor on my hay."

Joe nodded. "I'll go the extra dime. He's earned it."

"Put him in the stall at the end down there, the last one on the right."

"I have another question," Joe said. "Will it be all right if I lay down somewhere an' catch some shut-eye? I'm 'bout as wore out as the horse is."

The hostler, a bearded gent with a limp and a bad scar that covered much of the left side of his face, pointed toward a ladder that led to the hayloft overhead. "Help yourself.

I'm expecting a load of hay later on today, so you might want to pick a spot toward the back if you don't want to be stepped on up there." He smiled. "Of course, the cussing will likely wake you up anyway. It's hard work and small wages for pitching hay."

"You ever take in a fur trapper's rendezvous?" Joe asked.

"No, sir, I can't say that I have. Why?"

"Because you learn to sleep through plenty of noise at those things. It's only when some son of a bitch is tryin' to sneak up on me all quiet that I come awake. But noise, that don't bother me none."

"Then pick a spot up there and welcome."

"Thank you, friend. I'm beholden."

Joe stripped his saddle off the Palouse and turned it into the stall, where it promptly dropped to its knees and rolled, squirming in the dry straw. He dipped water from a trough behind the barn and filled a pail that he found in the stall. A small bunk in one corner of the stall was already full of good-quality grass hay—Joe pulled out a handful and smelled it to be sure. Then he gave the horse a half gallon of oats from a bin beside the tack room. While the animal ate, he scrubbed its back with a curry comb and completed the grooming with a soft dandybrush. When finally he was done settling the horse in for its rest, Joe gratefully climbed the ladder into the cavernous loft overhead.

The loft had hay piled on one side of the trapdoor, and straw on the other. Joe went to the far back end of the barn and stretched out on top of a pile of soft, sweet-smelling hay.

He was asleep practically before he had time enough to close his eyes.

"You Yankee son of a bitch!"

Joe woke to the sounds of scuffling feet and the thud of fists on flesh. He heard grunts of pain and the crash of breaking wood. It sounded like rendezvous all over again as he sat bold upright, tomahawk in hand to defend himself if need be.

The noise was coming from the barn floor below. There was no threat to him.

Someone, though, was getting the shit beaten out of him. The noises continued for several minutes, thumping and banging and muttered curses.

Whoever it was down there, this was not Joe's fight and he had no inclination to step in. Besides, he was not done sleeping.

Satisfied that no one was interested in his scalp, he returned the tomahawk to his sash, rolled over on his side, and prepared to go back to sleep.

"You can stop now," a different voice said. "I think you kil't him."

"Old bastard," another answered. "Serves him right."

"C'mon. Let's get outa here before someone sees us. No, dammit, not that way. We'll go out the back. Far as anybody knows, we ain't been here today." There was a slight pause, then, "Are you about damn done? I don't wanta be here when somebody comes."

"I'm done. Let's go."

Joe listened closely, wide awake now. The footsteps, like the voices, were those of two men. There was nothing distinctive about the footsteps, as there would have been had one of the men been the friendly hostler, but he would remember those voices.

Sure of what he would find even before he got down there, he went down the ladder to the floor beneath. The hostler lay slumped against the tack room wall. A pitchfork lay close by. The man's head was oddly shaped, the skull obviously crushed, probably by a heavy wooden bucket that lay in a corner several feet away from the body. The hostler's pockets were turned inside out.

That pissed Joe off. It was one thing to kill a man. Hell, he had killed plenty enough himself, some of them for reasons that others might not think justified. But petty theft to him was not a justifiable cause to kill.

He did not bother going over to touch the hostler or see if he was still breathing. He was not. Not with a head that looked like that. The eye on the good side of his face had popped halfway out of its socket, and was sightlessly staring toward the hayloft where Joe had just been. There was blood seeping out of the one ear that Joe could see, and a little from his nose and mouth as well.

The flies that can always be found around barns had abandoned the manure pile and were beginning to swarm to the corpse.

"Sorry, fellow," Joe said softly.

✛ 8 ✛

"**Y**OU! WHAT ARE you doing there?"

Joe turned to see who was shouting. It was a large man wearing sleeve garters and a derby hat. When he saw Joe looking at him, his voice rose into a shriek. "Help! Help! Murder! Help!"

Joe tried to walk outside and ask where he could find the local law so he could report this to somebody, but the man in the derby screamed again and fled before Joe could open his mouth to speak.

There were perhaps half-a-dozen people in view, and all the running and screaming certainly had their attention. Several of them started toward the livery, and within moments there were more citizens poking their heads out of windows and through doorways looking to see what the commotion was all about.

"He killed Sam. He killed Sam. That man. He done it. I

29

seen him standing over the body. He done it," the excitable fellow in the derby yelped.

"Now just hold on here a minute," Joe said soothingly to the first of the townspeople to arrive on the scene. "Don't get yourselves all het up here. I ain't done nothing for you t' be excited about."

"We'll see about that," said a tall, slender man wearing an apron. "Just don't be thinking you can get away. Just . . . just stand right there and don't move."

"I was just trying to . . ."

"Shut up, you piece of shit!" another man snarled.

Joe bristled at the son of a bitch's tone of voice as much as the language he used. "You got no call t' talk to me like that, damn you. Take it back or I'm like to bust your skull open."

It was, under the circumstances, a poor choice of words. He realized that—and regretted it—virtually as soon as the words left his tongue. Too late to call them back, though.

"Like you busted Sam's skull, is that it?"

People were crowding near now. Surrounding Joe. Staring at the hostler, whose named seemed to have been Sam something. Pressing closer and closer around Joe.

Had the Palouse been saddled, he would have made a break for it and tried to explain the truth afterward.

There were too many in the crowd now to fight.

Or anyway, too many for him to have a hope of winning a fight.

On the other hand, long odds had never stopped him before.

These town gents with their town ways might take him down—more than a few of them had guns in their hands—but they would not take him easy.

Joe balled his powerful hands into fists, raised his face to the sky, and let out a bloodcurdling savage war cry.

Blood at Bear Lake

The crowd parted before him.

Joe felt a moment of relief. Then another of puzzlement. Why would they—?

Then he saw.

A big man—a big man who happened to be wearing a star on his chest—was approaching. The man with the star held a double-barreled shotgun in his fists. It was for him that the crowd was melting back.

Not that Joe blamed them. He would gladly have gotten the hell out of the way of that scattergun, too, if he could. If the tubes of the damn thing didn't of a sudden swing right on line with his belly. If those twin hammers hadn't been eared back to what looked like full cock.

Joe Moss was willing to enter a fray with anybody or anything, either man or beast. But he would for damned sure rather *not* go up against a shotgun, thank you very much.

"I'm mighty glad you showed up here," Joe said as the lawman reached him. "There's been murder committed here, and I was wantin' to tell you about it."

The lawman grunted and glanced past Joe to the body that lay on the barn floor behind him.

Without warning, the butt end of the shotgun flashed around and connected with the side of Joe's head.

He heard a dull sound like a watermelon being dropped from a great height. For one brief instant, he had the sensation that he was falling, and then the world went suddenly dark.

✣ 9 ✣

"LORDY, MY HEAD hurts." Joe sat up. His head was pounding, throbbing in bumps and waves in time with his heartbeat. He felt worse than after a two-week-long drunk, an experience that he had come to know rather well in his rowdy youth.

"It ought to," a voice answered. "It was our blacksmith that clouted you. I deputized him to help bring you in peaceable. It worked, too. He laid you out right proper. There was a time when I wasn't at all sure you was gonna wake up again."

"What'd the son of a bitch hit me with? One of his hammers?"

"If he'd done that, he would have killed you sure. The butt of his shotgun was enough, but like Samson he did smite you a mighty blow."

"Remind me not to get in no fights with that man," Joe said. He blinked, having to struggle for a moment to convince his eyes that they should focus.

He was seated on the side of a steel platform that served as a bunk. There was no mattress, no pillow, no comforts. Between him and the man with the badge on his chest was a rank of floor-to-ceiling iron bars. The floor was paved with stone. But the walls were wood—sawed lumber, not logs—and there was a window. If it came to that, if these sons of bitches thought they were going to hang him or anything like that, Joe was fairly confident that he could get out. Eventually.

"Who are you?" he asked, careful not to move his head much when he spoke. This man with a star on his chest was not the same one he was starting to remember from before he was hit. That fellow had been burly and had a bushy beard. This one was slender, with a look of quickness and wiry strength. He was a little long in the tooth, though, for someone in the badge-packing business. Probably in his sixties, judging from his white, thinning hair and weathered features. He was clean-shaven except for a huge, carefully waxed and trimmed, snowy white mustache.

"My name is Tolbert Wilcox. I'm the town marshal."

"Your friends call you Bert?"

"It doesn't matter what my friends call me. You aren't one of them. You can call me Marshal Wilcox."

"Yes, sir." Joe took a deep breath and closed his eyes. To make him feel better, he imagined the sound of Marshal Wilcox's scalp ripping away from his head. It might be a pleasure to lift that hank of hair, he thought. And yes, the thought did make him feel better.

Joe smiled and opened his eyes. "I been out long?"

"Long enough. You slept the whole night through."

"I'll be damned," Joe said.

"You may well be. That is between you and the Lord. Do you want to see a preacher or a priest?"

"I didn't mean it that way," Joe said.

"I know the way you meant it, but the offer stands. If you want comfort, let me know. I'll have someone come in and read to you. Would you like a Bible? I allow the Good Book in my cells. Not much of anything else, though."

"Why am I here?" Then he remembered. The hostler at that livery. They thought he killed that man. "Hey, I'm innocent," Joe protested.

"In the eyes of the Lord we all are," Wilcox said, "but you are being judged by man."

"Judged? I didn' see much in the way o' judging out there. Those bastards woulda strung me up like a piñata an' laughed while I strangled."

"You will be judged in a duly constituted court of law. I will see to that. *Then* you will be hanged," Wilcox said. His smile held no mirth. "And if I have anything to do about it, the knot will come up behind your head and not beside it. Instead of your neck breaking to give you a quick end, you will indeed strangle slowly while you dance and gurgle. You see, Sam Farnsworth was a friend of mine and a deacon in our church."

"Farnsworth," Joe repeated. "That'd be the fella at the livery?"

"That's right, and a better man there never has been."

"Funny thing," Joe said. "I've noticed it time an' again. A man dies an' suddenly he's a saint. Might be a son of a bitch while he's alive, but soon as he goes belly-up, he's nigh onto bein' perfect."

"Sam was no sinner. He was a good man."

"Well, I got to admit," Joe said, "he was nice to me."

"Yet you killed him for the meager few dollars he had in his pockets."

"Is that what you figure happened?"

"Of course. I saw the body, you know. You turned his pockets inside out and took whatever you found there. It

34

could not have been much. Sam was not a wealthy man. Not in world terms, he was not."

"I seen the body," Joe agreed, "but I never touched him." He reached into his britches and turned his own pockets inside out. They were empty, of course. Taking everything out of them would be standard procedure. At least, it had been in every other jail Joe had ever been in. "You took my stuff. Did you find any small change when you did?"

"What do you mean?"

"I mean, think about it. A man running a business like that livery. What kinda money is he most likely to collect? Coins, right? Small change. Nickels, dimes, mostly quarters. D'you have a bank here in town?"

"What a strange question."

"Well, do you?"

"Have a bank? Yes. Of course we do."

"Ask the banker about this Sam fella's deposits. I bet he mostly came in with small change, maybe to turn in for currency or gold coin, but nobody likes t' walk around weighed down by ten pounds o' metal dragging at his pockets. An' there's not many customers will be paying a ten-cent bill with folding money. A livery deals mostly in small coin."

"I don't understand your point," the marshal said.

"My point is that you will not have found any such on me. You seem t' think I killed that man so I could rob him o' the few dollars he had on him. If that's so, where's them coins now? You didn't find more'n a couple small coins on me an' some gold coin an' currency. If I robbed that man, what d'you say I done with all his money?"

"You hid it perhaps."

Joe stood, his head aching all the more when he did so, and crossed the small cell to the bars that separated him from Wilcox. "Those folk thought they walked in on me in the commission of my crime. They thought I just done the killing. If that was so an' I intended to slip away before I was caught, I wouldn't of had time enough to hide all them coins. Nor, for that matter, no reason to. Remember, you're saying I was about to sneak off. If I done that, I surely woulda taken my loot with me. Fine. So where the fuck is it?" Joe demanded, his voice rising. "Did you find it on me? In my possibles bag? In my saddlebags? In my bedroll?"

"I haven't, uh . . ."

"You haven't looked in those? Haven't even looked?"

"Well, um . . ."

"You haven't. All right. Fine. Go look. Go through everything. You did bring it all in here when you brought me in, didn't you? So go take a look through it, then come back an' tell me what you found."

For the first time since Joe woke, Wilcox looked troubled. "I don't think . . ."

Whatever he intended to say, he changed his mind. He said nothing.

The marshal clamped his jaw shut, turned around, and left the cell area, closing a stout wooden door behind him.

✛ 10 ✛

J OE LOOKED UP at the sound of the door hinges creaking open. He had been sitting on the hard bunk—it was the only place in the cell where he could sit—trying to be patient.

It was a funny thing about that. When it came to waiting beside a game trail or waiting to ambush some son of a bitch who wanted to take his hair, Joe had the patience of a bronze statue. Yet when he was forced to deal with mental midgets like town folk, he had trouble forcing himself to hold still more than a few minutes at a time. Right now he wanted to rip the bars off this cell and hit somebody with them. Instead, he sat. And fumed.

Then the door opened and the marshal . . .

Damn! No Marshal Wilcox. Instead, it was a gray-haired, scrawny woman who came in, carrying a tray in one hand and both a key ring and a pewter pitcher in the other.

Joe immediately rose and tried to remove his hat, then remembered too late that he was not wearing one at the moment. "Ma'am." He nodded a greeting.

"Tolbert asked me to bring this to you. He would have brought it himself except he is meeting with the town council now."

"Yes, ma'am." Joe was not sure just why he was supposed to care about that. But whatever the woman had underneath the dish towel that covered her tray surely did smell good. It got his mouth to watering.

"Wait just a minute while I get the door unlocked. The tray won't fit through unless I open it."

"Yes'm."

The lady was in the cell area by herself, and by her own admission the marshal was nowhere near. She did not appear to be armed. If Joe wanted to break out, it would take only one backhanded blow to very likely break her neck.

But then, dammit, Joe was not much in favor of killing women. Not without provocation anyway. And this lady was smiling and fumbling with the tray, trying to balance it with one hand while she tried to manipulate the keys with the other. She scraped at the lock a little, but accomplished nothing except to spill a little coffee out of the pitcher she held in that same hand.

"Can I help you, ma'am?"

"Yes, please." And—incredibly—when he reached through the bars, she handed him not the tray, as he expected, but the key ring. "Can you reach through and unlock that for me, please?"

He did so easily enough, then stepped back and swung the door open.

"Thank you." She came in and carefully set the tray on the foot of the bunk, turning her back to Joe when she did so. He still had the jail keys in his hand. "There," she said when she straightened upright. "If there is anything else you need, call out. My name is Christine, by the way. I'm the marshal's wife."

"Pleased t' meet you, Miz Wilcox." Joe bobbed his head.

"Likewise, Mr. Moss." She smiled, then gathered her skirts. "I will leave you alone now so you can enjoy your dinner in peace."

"Yes, ma'am. Thank you."

Christine started for the cell door, but Joe stopped her, saying, "You might want t' take these with you, ma'am." He held out the key ring.

The lady shrugged her thin shoulders and giggled, then took the key ring and departed, carefully locking the cell door behind her.

Joe was puzzled. But not so much so that he failed to smile when he lifted the dish towel and saw what the marshal's lady had brought for his supper.

If all jail meals were this good, he might just arrange to get himself arrested more often.

✦ 11 ✦

WILCOX ENTERED THE cell block with a cat-that-ate-the-canary look about him. He was carrying the cell keys and a pair of handcuffs. "You and me need to take a little walk, Moss," he said as he unlocked the cell door.

Joe picked up the tray Mrs. Wilcox left behind—he had damn near polished it getting the last remnants of tasty gravy—and held it in both hands while the marshal rigged the cuffs rather loosely on Joe's wrists. "What about . . . ?" He gestured with the tray.

"Oops. I almost forgot." Wilcox took the tray in one hand, and with the other ushered Joe into the marshal's office. He set the tray aside and motioned toward the front door.

It was black night out there. With no windows in the cell block, Joe had lost track of the time. He had not thought it was so late, but obviously had been wrong about that.

"Where're we going, Marshal?"

"You'll see. It's right over there. Where all the lights are, do you see?"

"Yes, but . . ."

"Just go along here. You won't be sorry."

Wilcox certainly did not *act* like he was leading the goat to the slaughter. If anything, he seemed downright tickled with himself. Joe grunted and decided to "go along" just as the man asked. For the moment anyway.

The building with all the lights proved to be the meeting place for some sort of lodge, Joe guessed from the odd symbols and ornaments ranged around the walls. The place was one large long room, and it was virtually filled with townspeople, mostly men, but with a few women in the crowd as well.

At its head, there was a tall desk and in front of it a lectern. Chairs had been set to one side of the desk. Six of them. In the chairs were six plump gents wearing boiled shirts and fluffy neckties.

"Shit," Joe mumbled. He turned to the marshal and whispered, "They're a jury, ain't they?"

"Well, um, yes, Moss. They are indeed a jury of your peers."

"You cocksucker. You fooled me by bein' so easy. If I'd known what you was up to it woulda took you, the judge, and every one o' those sons o' bitches to pry me outa that cell and get me over here."

"I would appreciate it if you wouldn't use language like that. There are some ladies nearby who might overhear."

"Damn you," Joe said with considerable venom.

"Calm down and shut up. We have a trial to conduct here." The marshal reinforced his admonition by pulling a revolver out of his belt. Joe's own revolver, Joe noticed.

Gary Franklin

"Damn you," Joe repeated. But he allowed himself to be led to the lectern facing the big desk.

While he walked, however, he was looking around, thinking and planning. If he could just slip one hand free of the steel bracelets . . .

✦ 12 ✦

D AMN TRIAL WAS over before Joe had a chance to figure out how he was going to get away. It turned out
there were only two witnesses. One was the man who had
first walked into the livery barn and found Joe standing
over the dead man. The second was Marshal Wilcox.

"Every man here likely did business with Sam Farnsworth
some time or another. You likely paid him with a dime or a
quarter or even a handful of pennies. All Sam ever dealt in
was small money, then every week or so he would turn the
coins in for currency. Well, yesterday I checked with the
bank to see if Sam had changed his coins that morning. He
hadn't. And Moss here didn't have no pocketful of coins
neither. He had a tidy amount of folding money, but not
much in the way of coins."

Wilcox dropped his chin and folded his arms. He
looked from one end of the row of jurors to the other, then

spoke again. "Do you know what that tells me? *This man is innocent.* We have wrongly accused him, and I say we have to vote him innocent in this duly constituted court of law. We have to turn him loose with apology."

Joe blinked, not at all sure he correctly heard what it was that he just in fact did hear.

The judge banged the desk with his gavel. The prosecutor called for a show of hands of all those who thought Joe was guilty. Not a single hand went up.

"Innocent?" the prosecutor said.

All six hands were lifted.

Wilcox grinned and turned to Joe. "That makes it legal. You've been exonerated proper and can't be charged with that crime again. Even if you confessed to it now, you couldn't be charged."

"Well, that ain't gonna happen for the simple reason I didn't do it." Joe shook his head. "But damn, Marshal, you coulda told me what was happening beforehand. I was some worried up till I realized what you was up to there."

"Sorry." Wilcox grinned. "But it was more fun this way."

"You was putting on a show for the whole town, wasn't you?"

The marshal shrugged. "Partly maybe. Another reason is that I wanted the real killers to start sweating. Now they know they didn't get clean away. And worried men make mistakes."

"Marshal, it's been my experience that it's mostly stupid men who do stupid crimes t' begin with. I suggest you look at the dumber end o' the scale when you go to looking for the killers."

"I know I am in no position to ask you for favors, Moss, but I am going to ask anyway."

"You can ask. Don't know as I'll agree to whatever it is you're asking for, though."

"The thing is," the marshal said, "you are the only witness we have to Sam's murder."

"I never saw . . ."

"I know, I know, you didn't actually see. But you say you did hear voices. You might recognize something that you don't even realize you know. The thing is, Moss, I would like for you to pin a deputy's badge on your chest and help me ferret out whoever killed Sam.

"And while I happen to know that you don't really need the money, the job pays a dollar and a half a day."

"An' keep?" Joe asked. He smiled. "Does your wife's good cooking come along with the deal?"

"If that's what it takes to get your cooperation, then yes, it does."

Joe fingered his chin. He wanted to find Fiona. But it was still possible that she was on her way here right now and simply had not yet made it.

Before he went sashaying off into the hills looking under every bush in the faint hope of finding her, it only made sense that he wait and give Fiona time to get here if this indeed was where she was bound.

He nodded. "I'll take the job, Marshal. For now. I'll leave when I reckon I need to."

"That's fair enough," Wilcox said. "Call me Tolbert if you like, Joe. Now come with me over to the jail. We'll get your weapons out of the locker and put that star on your shirt."

"Uh, Tolbert?"

"Yes, what is it, Joe?"

Joe extended his hands toward the marshal. They still were shackled with the handcuffs.

Wilcox grinned and smacked himself in the forehead. Then he dug into his pocket for the key that would open the manacles.

Joe thought he might possibly—just barely possibly—have been able to slip the cuffs and make an escape from there.

But he was glad he hadn't had to try, especially with what looked like an entire town full of armed men on hand if he did make a break for it. No, sir, he was mighty glad.

✢ 13 ✢

JOE ACCOMPANIED TOLBERT Wilcox to the marshal's home, a small house set two blocks off the main street of Lake's Crossing. Christine Wilcox met them at the door. She took her husband's hat and gun belt and hung them on a peg by the front door where they would be handy to grab in a hurry if need be.

Joe took the hint and draped his belt and hat there, too. But he kept his bowie and tomahawk in his sash. He would have felt naked without those. Besides, how do you hang a tomahawk on a wooden peg anyway?

"Would you like pie and coffee?" she offered.

"Just the coffee," Tolbert said. "We'll take it in the front room. We need to talk some business here, Christine."

"I'll bring it straightaway," she responded, obviously taking the hint that the menfolk would not be socializing and her presence was not really welcome. "Gentlemen." She pointed toward a small room that was filled nearly to

47

overflowing with a sofa and two huge, deep upholstered armchairs, all of it in matching dark blue fabric.

"Thank you, ma'am."

Christine disappeared toward the back of the house. Joe waited for Tolbert to settle into his favored armchair, this one with a lamp on a stand that placed it over his left shoulder. The lamp was lighted and a reflector angled to Tolbert's liking. There was also a low side table placed nearby with a glass humidor and supply of matches beside it.

"Do you smoke, Joe?"

"Yes, I do."

"Feel free to light up. This tobacco isn't bad. A little old, but I haven't allowed it to dry out." That was a problem lately. With war raging back East, the usual flow of tobacco from the Southern states was cut off, and both the quality and quantity of the available West Indian tobacco was lacking. Tolbert selected a pipe from among several waiting on a stand beside the humidor.

Joe thanked the man and dug his own pipe out of his possibles pouch. He filled it with Tolbert's tobacco and helped himself to a match. By the time he had his pipe drawing nicely—Tolbert was right about the tobacco being a cut above the usual—Christine was there with coffee. She set the cups down and silently withdrew.

"In a way," Tolbert mused, "I almost wish we had gone ahead and convicted you of Sam's murder, Joe."

"But I really didn't . . ."

"Oh, I know you didn't do it. That isn't what I meant. The thing that's worrying me now, Joe, is that your innocence means that this community still has a murderer running around loose somewhere."

"Two," Joe said.

"Two what?"

"Two murderers."

"You're sure about that?"

Joe nodded and puffed on his pipe. "Positive. I heard two voices, and they weren't one guy talking to himself. There was two of them as robbed an' killed that man."

Tolbert grunted and sat in silence for a moment. Joe sipped at the steaming hot coffee. It was a little bitter with age from sitting on the stove too long, but he had surely drunk worse.

"You have to help me find them," Tolbert said after a brief silence. "We can't let Sam's murderers slip away. I suppose the first thing I should do is to see can I figure out has anyone suddenly left town without saying anything about it ahead of time." He puffed on his pipe. "Most folks around here are friendly. They don't have anything to hide. Nothing real serious anyway. They would've mentioned it if a trip was planned."

Tolbert laid his pipe aside, crossed his legs, and laced his hands over his knee. "For right now, though, Joe, I'd like you to tell me, nice and slow, every least detail you can remember about those murderers. Everything you heard and everything you saw. Everything. Can you do that? Will you?"

"Gladly," Joe said. He set in to do exactly that.

✢ 14 ✢

J OE SPENT THE night in a cluttered toolshed, a lean-to attached to the back of Wilcox's house. Christine apolo-
gized for the rough surroundings, but Joe grinned and
waved off her apologies. "You should oughta see some o'
the places I've slept. But then come to think of it, it's better
that a nice lady like you don't know."

He slept well—and free—and as usual woke well before
dawn. The Wilcoxes apparently were not such early risers,
so Joe pumped a basin full of cold water and washed on
the back porch. He slicked his hair back with his hands,
checked the set of his Colt revolver and the tomahawk and
bowie, then wandered into town in search of a café that was
open at the early hour. Preferably one with a handsome
lady handling the orders.

Joe was married—Lordy, what a strange thought that
was; he did not know if he would ever get over the magic of

it—and he would never stray. But there was nothing wrong with a man liking to just *look*.

He found a likely place two blocks down and three over from the marshal's house. Yellow lamplight streamed from the street-side windows, giving the café a cheery look about it.

Until Joe walked inside, that is.

Cheery? Not damn likely.

There were only two customers and a fat, greasy cook inside the place. The cook was sweating from the heat of his stove, and both customers were huddled over their plates like they thought someone was going to come along and snatch their food away.

The cook tended his stove and the customers plied their forks, all in silence except for the clatter of the firebox door when the cook added wood to his stove and the scrape-scrape-scrape of steel fork tines on pewter plates.

Joe took a seat at the low counter and turned upright the tin cup that had been laid out there placed upside down. The cook came over to him.

"Coffee?"

"Please. And I reckon I could stand some breakfast, too. What I'd like is . . ."

"Never mind what you'd like. If you want breakfast, all you gotta do is say so and take what I give you."

"An' that would be exactly what?" Joe asked.

"Slice of pork. Mess of fried 'taters. An' all the mush an' syrup you can eat. An' that coffee that's in front of you."

"No eggs?"

"Do I look like a chicken?"

Joe thought about suggesting that, no, the fellow did not look like a chicken but he did closely resemble a pig. But hell, he had come in here for a meal, not a fight. He choked back that response and said, "That sounds all right. How much?"

"Quarter."

Joe nodded. "I'm in."

He sat back and sipped the coffee, which was better than he expected. Maybe he would be pleasantly surprised about the rest of the breakfast here, too.

While he waited, he went back over what little he knew about Sam Farnsworth's killers. It was little enough. Just the sounds of some scuffling and two voices. No names. Nothing unusual enough in either the movements or the talking that he could pin down for someone else to recognize.

A few noises. And a dead man left lying in the dirt of a livery barn floor.

Joe wouldn't say that he had gotten to know Sam Farnsworth, but the man had been decent to him. And somewhere, Farnsworth likely had family. Now they might never know what became of him. He might simply have vanished in the vastness of the West.

Like Fiona. God! Fiona.

Where was she this morning?

Was she riding her sorrel mare up here even now, heading for the home of her photographer friend?

While he waited for his food, Joe closed his eyes and in the privacy of his mind chanted a plea of supplication to the gods of the Lakota and the Blackfoot.

He did not open his eyes again until a rich, warm aroma filled his nostrils, and the cook set a pewter plate down in front of him.

Joe smiled then.

He knew what he wanted to do when he got back to Tolbert's house.

✣ 15 ✣

B Y THE TIME Joe finished his breakfast, the sun was almost clear of the horizon and people were beginning to
stir around town, heading to their places of work, opening
shops, and preparing for the day to come.

Joe ducked into an alley and managed—he hoped—to get
back to Tolbert's house without anyone paying attention to
him. More to the point, he got there without having to see too
closely any of the local folks who were out on the streets now.

He was grinning when Christine Wilcox let him in at the
back door. "You're just in time for breakfast," she told him.

"Oh, I've already had mine, but I want t' talk with Tolbert, thanks."

"Then sit down. That chair over there if you don't mind.
Tolbert always sits here. Coffee?"

"Please." Times when Joe would refuse a cup of coffee—
or a glass of something stronger—were rare. He took the
seat she indicated, dropping his hat onto the floor under it.

"I'll get my husband." She poured coffee for Joe before she disappeared into another room, presumably to tell Tolbert that they had company. When she came back, she began filling a plate. "He will be right out."

"Thank you, ma'am."

Christine set the plate onto the table, poured coffee at that place, and left the kitchen. Tolbert came in a moment later in undershirt and galluses. He had a dab of shaving soap under his jaw. The soap dangled free and wobbled when he spoke. "Good morning, Joe. Sleep well?"

"Yes, sir."

"Are you ready to put that badge on and start deputying?"

Joe smiled. "Deputying. Is that a word?"

"If it isn't, then it oughta be. You ready?"

"I'm ready enough, but if you don't mind a suggestion, I'd like to lay one out for you."

"Oh, I'll listen to most anything. We'll see where I take it from there."

"D'you know the best way to trap a mountain lion, Tolbert, or a big tom bobcat?"

"What has . . . no, Joe, I wouldn't know about that."

"You want to bait them in, Tolbert. An' the best bait for a lion is a plain, ordinary kitten. A house cat if you can find one."

"A kitten?"

"Yes, sir. I used t' know men who would buy or trap all the kittens they could find before they left Saint Louie and carry them into the mountains in cages. Stake one o' them down and lay your traps out . . . you're damn sure"—Joe remembered too late where he was and gave a worried glance toward the doorway to make sure Christine had not overheard strong language—"you are gonna pull in any lion within earshot. You set your traps an' let the lions come to you."

"That is interesting, Joe, but what—?"

"I'm getting' to that, Tolbert. What I have in mind is for you t' set the trap, then sit back an' let our murderers come in to the bait."

"I assume you don't intend to stake out a kitten to make this happen."

"No, sir, what I have in mind is for you t' use a drunk for bait. A passed-out drunk."

Wilcox scowled. "What in the world good would that do?"

Joe's grin flashed bright. He sat back in his chair and took a swallow of Christine's good coffee before he answered.

"It depends on who the drunk is. And does word get around town that he can identify the killers. Which he will surely do, quick as he sobers up from the toot he's on to celebrate getting out o' that jail."

"The drunk would be you, I take it?"

"Yes, sir. An' I think it would be a nice touch if I was t' do my passing out over in Sam Farnsworth's stable. I figure to wait until the streets are busy, then carry a bottle in my hand an' stagger over there to that barn. Me and my Colt's revolving pistol."

"I could give you time to get over there, then make my rounds. I could grumble about you getting drunk before I had time to get that identification from you," Wilcox mused.

Joe slapped the table so hard a dish bounced and the cutlery rattled. "Exactly!"

Wilcox smiled. "I like it."

"I don't happen to have a whiskey bottle with me, so you might wanta go over to a saloon right after breakfast and fetch one. You can start complaining then about your new deputy going on a all-night drinking bender. Won't nobody know the difference. The word can start getting around right away."

"Is there anything else I can do to help?"

"No. Just plant the bait for me. Then come over to the livery once the shooting is over so's you can collect the bodies."

"Joe. If you can arrest the killers without any further bloodshed, it is your obligation to do that. You must try, do you understand me?"

Joe nodded. And smiled. Take them alive. Sure he understood that. Sure he did.

✦ 16 ✦

IT WASN'T ALL that much different from waiting beside a
game trail. Either way, you picked your spot and kept still.

Joe sprinkled a little whiskey on himself, dribbling it
onto his shirt and rubbing it over his face and in his hair.
He just hoped the smell stayed with him long enough to attract the quarry he was after today. Human quarry, but that
didn't matter. It was not the first time.

He decided it would be best to wait inside one of the stalls.
The walls were tall enough to pretty much guarantee that
any would-be assassin would come at him by way of the
stall door. He wouldn't have to worry about anyone coming
at him from the back.

Before he set his trap, he climbed into the loft where he
had been sleeping when this whole thing got started. He
kicked a goodly amount of straw through the ladder opening, then climbed down again and used a pitchfork—the
same pitchfork Sam Farnsworth tried to defend himself

with—to transfer the straw into the stall he'd chosen. After all, there was no need to be uncomfortable while he waited, and it wouldn't hurt to have some straw to burrow into.

He mounded the straw in a far corner and moved a pair of mules out of the stall across the aisle, putting them into the corral in back. Once the shooting started, he did not want to have to worry about a stray bullet harming one of the mules.

"There y' go, boys," he said as he turned them loose inside the enclosure. "Just don't tell on me if anybody comes along, eh?"

Chuckling, Joe returned to the livery barn and took his position in the pile of straw.

He wiggled this way and that for a few minutes to get comfortable, then drew his revolver and shoved it under the straw close to his hand. In that hand he very loosely held the cherrywood haft of his tomahawk. The big bowie was close to hand in his sash.

He laid the whiskey bottle he had very publicly carried over here on its side close to his hip. On the way over, he had staggered and made a show of being drunk.

The new deputy, newly acquitted on a charge of murder, was going on a toot. Joe smiled to himself. Yeah, word about that ought to get around mighty quick.

"You boys can come along any ol' time now," Joe mumbled softly in the silence of the big barn.

He lay back against the wall, pillowed there by the straw pile.

There was silence all around him, but in the theater of his mind he could again see Fiona. Lovely Fiona coming naked out of that nameless creek back in Nebraska Territory, moonlight reflecting on the water that streamed from her. Then the feel of her skin, cold from the creek water, goose bumps cobbling the flesh of her breasts. But not cold, not at all cold lower down.

Blood at Bear Lake

Fiona, shy as a virgin on their wedding night, her beautiful body hidden from his adoring gaze. Hidden at first, that is. The shyness had gone. And so had the sleeping dress.

Oh, he could remember . . .

Outside the barn, the slow commerce of an ordinary day clip-clopped past.

"Come on in," Joe whispered softly in the dusty silence of the barn. "Come t' me, boys," he said, too softly to be heard by any other ear. "Come kill me if you can."

✢ 17 ✢

THE DUMB SONS of bitches probably thought they were being quiet. They should have taken some lessons.

Joe had been stalked by Shoshones, Snakes, Cheyenne, and grizzly bears. He had been charged, ambushed, and more than once called out for one-on-one hand-to-hand combat. He had been fought with rifle, arrow, knife, and claw. He still had his hair.

No, if these boys wanted to take a scalp, they should have started with something easier. Like a toddler in short pants.

He heard them whispering before they even reached the back doors, which he had left open for their convenience. He couldn't make out what they were saying, and wouldn't have cared to listen to their bullshit and bravado even if he could hear.

That was all the talking was: bullshit and bravado. They were working themselves up to murder. The murder of a man they thought was drunk and defenseless, yet still they had to work themselves up to it.

Pathetic assholes, Joe thought with contempt. They were not worthy of his abilities. It would be too easy to kill them.

Not that he would hesitate when the moment came. Even a newborn rattlesnake has venom.

Joe waited patiently, eyes half closed so that he was looking past lowered lids, fingers wrapped lightly around the haft of his trusty old tomahawk.

In years of meat hunting and mortal combat, Joe had had misfires of both rifles and pistols, but the tomahawk and the bowie knife never misfired.

He could hear the scrape of shoe soles on the hard-packed floor of the stable and the soft back and forth flow of whispers and exhortations.

These were not deliberate killers and they were frightened, he realized. He could practically smell the stink of their fear as they entered the alleyway between the rows of stalls and came near.

". . . you do . . ."

". . . old ma . . ."

"I'll take . . . you . . . then we . . ."

They were moving even slower now. They had no idea which stall he was in, or for that matter whether he had entered any of the stalls. Idiots! He had left the damn stall door ajar so they could figure it out without pissing themselves. But they crept along, whispering, peeking over stall walls, probably trembling with mingled fear and excitement.

"There. The old bastard's in this'un here. He's passed clean out. Take a look."

There was a moment of silence and some bumps and scrapes, enough to wake any warrior Joe had ever known and any mountain man, too. Or anyway, all who survived.

Anyone who could sleep though this much warning was dead certain to lose his hair to Injuns.

"We'll go in an' I'll count to three. We'll both of us fire on the count o' three."

Joe appreciated the information. They had guns. Why the simpletons would not stand where they were and try to put lead into him, he did not pretend to understand. Hell, wasn't the whole idea of a gun to let its user take down a target from a distance? These assholes were so unsure of themselves that they wanted to be standing over their victim so they could fire at point-blank range.

That knowledge swept away any sense of regret Joe might have had about taking their lives.

He had been tempted to begin with. A little bit. After all, they likely hadn't meant to murder Sam Farnsworth. They'd only wanted to rob Sam. And when they did kill him, it was by beating him to death. That was something that was not apt to've been planned ahead of time. It was something that simply happened in the heat of the moment.

But this time they had acquired guns—bought with the money they took from Sam's still-warm body perhaps—and brought them with the deliberate intent to kill the man they believed could identify them.

Fine. Come closer, boys. Come closer, Joe thought.

The hinges of the stall door creaked, and after a few moments the door swung open.

The murderers came forward, moving on tiptoe just as quietly as they knew how.

Joe was surprised. He'd expected a couple of shabby layabouts. Drifters or grifters or ne'er-do-wells.

These boys were nicely dressed in suits and boiled shirts. They wore derby hats and smelled lightly of bay rum, suggesting it had not been long since they were shaved.

Well dressed or not, they were already murderers, and they intended to murder again.

That was one thing. *But Joe Moss was the man they proposed to murder.*

Joe let out an ear-shattering and, more importantly, unnerving roar as he rose to a sitting position, his right arm already moving and the never-fail tomahawk flashing.

As soon as the tomahawk left his hand, he was reaching for the big bowie at his waist.

The 'hawk had time to make only a half turn before it buried itself in the breastbone of the nearer attacker. It entered his chest just to the left of a black onyx shirt stud, and the white shirt was quickly flooded with scarlet.

Joe leaped to his feet, the bowie flashing in his hand. Chopping once and then slashing.

The second would-be killer screamed. Joe's first chop with the heavy bowie severed his hand at the wrist so that it dangled from the stump by only a thin strip of flesh. Blood pumped out where the hand used to be, and from his belly—opened up by Joe's slash with the razor-sharp knife—coils of gray gut spilled out onto the floor.

The kid shrieked again and collapsed beside his companion, who was already on the floor, either dead or soon would be.

The second one sat on the ground trying to gather his guts and push them back inside his belly, using one hand and the stump where the other had been.

If Joe had been a merciful sort of man, he likely would have done that one the favor of relieving him of his agony by way of a bullet in the back of the brain or a quick swipe of the bowie across his jugular.

But Joe was in no mood for mercy with these two. They'd murdered one man and would cheerfully have stood by while

Joe hung for their crime—he remembered seeing them in the crowd that assembled calling for his head—and today they'd wanted to murder him when they thought he was drunk and defenseless.

Mercy? Maybe from God if they asked for it. But not from Joe Moss.

He picked up the fallen pistol from the floor beside the gutted son of a bitch—there was no sense letting him get hold of it so he could put a bullet in his own brain—and tossed it aside.

"Now count to three, you asshole," he snarled at the boy who now just sat there, cradling a pile of gut in his one good hand.

Then Joe turned and went to find Marshal Wilcox. There likely would be paperwork and such to take care of after a civilized killing. Wilcox would know more about that shit than Joe ever wanted to.

✢ 18 ✢

"Jesus Christ, Joe, you shouldn't ought to have done that."

"They were coming to kill me, Tolbert. I was just defending myself. A man's got a right t' do that."

"I don't mean about you killing them, Joe. Everybody knows you had no choice about that. I mean about . . . about you scalping them after. Especially since the murderers were these boys—with such powerful fathers. Merle Esrig is an important man in this town, and the idea of him standing there . . . watching . . . while you lifted his own son's hair . . . Jesus, Joe!"

"I waited till they was dead, Tolbert. I thought that was more'n considerate enough."

"Well, I can tell you this, Joe. You are not a popular man in this town right now, and the way those boys' fathers feel, I can't be responsible for what they might do."

"They might hire somebody t' come after me, you mean," Joe said. It was not really a question.

Wilcox shrugged, but did not directly answer.

"You want me t' get out o' town, is that it?"

"Yes, Joe, I'm afraid so."

"What happened t' me being your deputy for the next little while?"

"Merle is on the town council. There is no way in this world he would allow you to draw pay from the town. Besides, Sam's murder has been cleared up. You did that. We will . . . I'll pay you something out of my own pocket, Joe. Don't worry about that."

"Oh, hell, Tolbert, it ain't money that I'm thinking of. I got enough money. Reckon I can earn me some more comes the time I need it. It's just that I got a reason why I want to hang around here a spell longer."

Fiona. She might yet be headed here, expecting to hide out with the photographer Faxon Roderus and his wife. She had hidden there before Joe found and married her. If she returned now, Joe wanted to be here to meet her.

On the other hand, it was equally true that she could be going almost anywhere so long as it was not Virginia City, where Peabody had placed a price on her lovely head.

Joe simply did not know where she was or what she intended. They had not had time, nor had they foreseen the need, to discuss alternate plans before they were attacked by Peabody's armed thugs back at St. Mary of the Mountain, and once the bullets started flying, there was no choice but for Fiona to make her escape while Joe held off the attackers.

Now he could only pray that, wherever she was, she was safe from harm.

"I'm sorry, Joe. I really am," Wilcox said, bringing Joe back to the here and now.

"Oh, I ain't blaming you, Tolbert."

"You just can't . . . This is a civilized town, Joe, filled with folks most of whom have never seen anything more violent than two schoolkids fighting at recess. And for you to take the scalps off two upstanding young men of the community . . ."

"Upstanding?"

"Their fathers are anyway."

"Don't let it slip your mind that those 'upstanding' young fellas murdered another upstanding member o' the community, Tolbert."

"Believe me, I do remember that. It is the reason you are not in jail right now for killing them. But the fact remains, you will have to leave town. You simply must."

"All right, dammit, but can I at least have time t' go over to the general store an' resupply? There's some other shit I want t' get, too."

"Do it in a hurry, Joe. I want you away from here before the sun sets behind that mountain yonder."

"An' if I'm not?"

"There might well be bloodshed, Joe."

"You know as well as I do, Tolbert, that if there's more blood spilled over this matter, I'll do my level best t' see that it ain't mine. An' if I do say so, I'm pretty good at killing."

"And raising hair afterward. Yes, I know that."

"I'll leave quick as I'm done making my purchases, Tolbert. You have my word on it."

"All right, I . . . I'm sorry, Joe. Real sorry."

Joe offered his hand, and Marshal Tolbert Wilcox accepted it. "Good-bye, Joe. Good luck."

✠ 19 ✠

JOE TOOK A step backward and grunted as he surveyed the pile of goods on the store counter. "Add a quarter pound o' horseshoe nails and that should do me when it comes to supplies, but there's some more items I'll be wanting, too. Is that a Hudson's Bay blanket I see up there?"

"Y-yes, sir." The clerk kept looking at Joe as if he expected the former mountain man to scalp him like he had those young men.

"I'll have the blanket, then. And a Henry rifle. I lost the one I used to have and I favor them. Reckon I'd like another."

"A Henry? Oh, my. That is one of those newfangled repeaters, isn't it? I've heard about those but never saw one. Sorry, but I don't have a Henry to sell you. I do have a pair of Spencer carbines you could choose from." The man shrugged. "Ever since the war back East . . . The army issues a good many of these Spencers, and after a battle people come along and scavenge up all the lost and fallen weapons. The muskets are popular because they hit so hard. On the other hand, there's lots of them available. You can buy a decent musket for half a dollar. A Spencer in good shape is ten dollars. Lord knows what one of those Henrys would cost."

"You got ammunition for the Spencer?"

"Yes, sir. It's fairly common."

"Let me see what you have."

The clerk laid two of the stubby little carbines on the counter, then picked up one of them and held it muzzle-downward. "You see this thing in the butt plate? Well, you turn it . . . like so . . . and pull it out . . . like this. This tube has a spring in it. You just drop the cartridges, up to seven at a time, into here, then push the tube in behind." He closed the loading gate and upended the Spencer.

"The cartridges feed from underneath. You work the trigger guard like you would use the lever on a Henry. Down, then up again. And your cartridge is loaded."

"What about the hammer? When you moved that lever, nothing happened to cock the hammer."

"You have to cock the hammer yourself."

"My Henry carried more cartridges."

"True." The man smiled. "But I don't have a Henry to sell you. I do have these Spencers. And the Spencer cartridge is fifty-six caliber. Your Henry was, what, forty-something?"

Joe nodded. "Forty-four."

"Do you want the Spencer?"

"Yeah, I'll take one of 'em." Joe picked up the one nearer him—the little gun was surprisingly heavy—and examined it closely, then did the same with the other. He weighed them for a moment, one in each hand, as if considering buying them by the pound, then firmly said, "This one." He laid the other back on the counter.

"You will want ammunition, of course."

"Yeah. Couple hundred rounds should do."

"Two hundred rounds? Gracious." The clerk chuckled. "Are you going to war that you need all that?"

"Could damn well be that I will, not that it's anything to you," Joe snapped.

"Oh, I . . . I'm sorry. I didn't mean anything by that."

"Just give me the ammunition an' figure out what I owe you for all this. I got a horse and a mule tied outside to pack it on."

"Yes, sir. Right away, sir."

The clerk helped him carry his purchases out onto the sidewalk, then left Joe to the task of building a balanced load out of it all.

The mule was one he had taken from the corral behind Sam Farnsworth's livery barn. Joe figured there was no one alive to dispute his right to take the animal. And, dammit, the town owed him something for his deputy work, whether they liked it or not.

If someone wanted to object, let them. In the meantime, he needed a pack animal. Besides, he had a fondness for mules anyway. They were ugly sons of bitches but tough. Joe liked that about them.

By the time he got everything sorted out and loaded onto the pack frame—which he'd also appropriated from the livery barn—it was nearing sundown. Not the best time of day to start a journey, but Joe did not want to cause any more problems for Tolbert Wilcox than he already had.

He snapped a long lead to the mule's bit ring and climbed onto the Palouse.

"Boys, I got no damned idea where we're going next. But we need to find Fiona, so let's get on with it."

He touched his heels to the sides of the Palouse and started riding.

✛ 20 ✛

IF IT HAD been up to him, Joe would have liked to stay in Lake's Crossing a few more days. There was still a chance Fiona would head there hoping to stay with the friends she was living with when Joe finally found her after their years of forced separation. But the Fates decreed otherwise when Joe was "invited" to leave town. Well, maybe those Fates had some reason to move him along against his will.

Sometimes, he thought his whole damned life was taking place beyond his will.

Then he grinned. Some of it, of course. But not all.

If there was one thing he could say about himself, it was that he was a free man and had lived a mighty good life. He had traveled far and seen some wonderful things. Drunk some fine whiskey . . . and plenty of bad. Bedded some splendid women . . . and plenty of bad. Had some good fights . . . and some not so good. And managed to keep on wearing his own hair through it all.

Gary Franklin

Now he had a beautiful wife and a sweet daughter. Oh, he looked forward to the time when he could get properly acquainted with Jessica, to the time when the three of them would be a family together.

That would happen just as soon as he could find Fiona again and the two of them could reclaim Jessica from the nuns back in Carson City.

But . . . where to look? How to find her?

Joe rode a few miles outside Tolbert Wilcox's jurisdiction and made camp, making no effort to hide his presence there. If any of those hidebound sons of bitches who threw him out of town wanted to come after him—let them. He wouldn't mind adding a few scalps to the collection already in his war bag.

He made some dough and rolled it between his palms to form long strips, then wound them around dingle sticks and baked them over the flames of a small fire, not waiting for the fire to burn down to coals.

Joe slept with his tomahawk held loose in one hand and the Colt revolver in his belt. Breakfast the next morning was creek water and leftover stick bread. Then he used the tomahawk to make a blaze on the trunk of a large cottonwood.

He pulled the Spencer carbine out of its scabbard and counted off a hundred paces from the cottonwood tree.

Loading the magazine of the Spencer the way the clerk showed him, Joe worked the trigger guard—the movement seemed a little awkward to him, but he knew he would get used to it—and cocked the hammer. Aimed and quickly fired. Pushed the trigger guard lever down and yanked it back up. Aimed. Fi—dammit! He had forgotten to cock the hammer. With his Henry, using the lever did that job at the same time. He tried again. Cocked. Fired.

Then he walked forward and critically examined where the bullets struck. The Spencer, he judged, shot just a little bit high and a hair to the left. That was all right. Now that he knew where it shot, he could compensate. And when he got where he was going, he could borrow some tools and correct the sights.

When he got where he was going.

Last night when he went to bed, he'd had no idea where it was that he intended to search for Fiona. Now he did.

His nighttime pondering reminded him that the last place he'd seen Fiona before their recent reunion was outside Fort Laramie. That was where her sonuvabitch father had forced them apart five years ago. In the little time he and Fiona spent together since their reunion and marriage, Joe had often spoken of his friendship with Sol Pennington, a former mountain man who ran a trading post at Fort Laramie. Maybe Fiona would head for Fort Laramie in the expectation of finding her husband there.

He hated the thought of a woman traveling alone on the Salt Lake emigrant route, but he knew Fiona to be courageous. Perhaps more so than was good for her.

If she thought she might find Joe at the other end of that road, Joe knew she would set out on it regardless of the dangers she would face. From Indians. From drought and heat. From renegade whites who thought that the absence of civilized surroundings meant they no longer had to act like civilized men. The dangers were boundless, as Joe knew full well. He also knew that Fiona would be willing to face them.

His hope now was that he could find her before any harm befell his brave and beautiful bride.

Joe reloaded the magazine of the Spencer and shoved it back into the leather, then saddled his Palouse and loaded the mule ready to travel.

Of a sudden, he was anxious to get moving.

He wanted more than ever—more than anything—to find Fiona.

✢ 21 ✢

J OE SAW THE dust long before he ever saw them, and
heard the jangle of their trace chains and the screech
and squeal of axles that needed grease long before they
ever came near. Not many wagons, he thought, but they
were in bad condition. Another ragtag bunch of ignorant
emigrants, he figured. Likely half-starved, too. More
simple-minded pieces of human shit too stupid to wipe
their own asses. Well, they could just go along on the
damned trail without his help. Damned if he was going to
bother trying to educate the dumb sons of bitches. No, sir.

Grumbling and groaning under his breath, Joe stood
from beside his tiny campfire and poured more water into
his battered coffeepot—damned if he was going to add
fresh grounds for a bunch of pork eaters so ignorant they
didn't know enough to grease a wagon wheel—and moved
the pot over the flames.

He had been on the road three days now and this would

be the third outfit he passed, all of them headed toward California. And away from the war.

The war was bad, they said. It had gone past armies in uniform fighting each other. Now it was neighbor shooting at neighbor. The folks he'd seen thus far were mostly from Missouri and Tennessee and they were more escaping from something than going toward anything. They traveled out of desperation instead of hope. Joe could see that in their eyes.

Not that he was going to be bothered with them. The wagon tracks of those who had gone before were plain enough that a blind man couldn't get lost in this vast expanse of rolling hills and runty cedar scrub. The hell with them one and all.

But they would likely be hungry, damn them for a nuisance. He took out his bowie and eyed the antelope he had knocked down earlier in the afternoon. He would slice off just a little to give to the stupid bastards. A haunch maybe. Or . . . what the hell. He could always get more. Let them take this whole antelope. The meat would just go bad before he could be bothered with drying it anyway. Might as well give it to the fools from back East as see it rot and go to waste.

He added wood to his fire.

Joe was standing with coffee boiling and meat to offer when the wagons rolled ponderously into view.

There were only two of them, drawn by gaunt oxen. Three on one wagon. Only two on the other. He could see from the way the wagon wheels cut into the soil that the wagons were much too heavily loaded. It amazed him that anyone so ignorant could have gotten this far. And by themselves, too, without the support of others.

A proper train should consist of half a hundred outfits or more. For protection, of course, but even more for the diversity of skills that could be found in a large train. Out away from the towns and the farms back East, a good many of these movers were as helpless as babes. They needed one another's abilities to make a functioning whole.

But a small outfit like this . . . Joe shook his head and waited for them to reach him.

Of the five oxen, two looked ready to drop right then. And he doubted that more than the one pale red near wheeler on the first wagon would make it all the way across the Sierras. These people needed to find themselves a nice place to hole up until their animals could recover some strength after the ordeal of the desert.

"Howdy."

"Howdy yer own self." The man who seemed to be the leader of this tiny band came forward and stuck his hand out. "Name's Howard Wickersham."

"Joe Moss." He took the offered handshake.

"These is my brothers, Tom and Benjamin. We's from Missoura. Would you be Yankee or Secesh?"

"Neither one," Joe said. "Not that it's any nevermind o' yours, Mr. Wickersham."

"Everybody says that, y' know. Nobody ever means it. Now us Wickershams, we's for the Union." Wickersham, a man almost as gaunt as his oxen, cocked his head and peered at Joe expectantly, obviously waiting for some sort of response to that admission.

Joe had none to give. He did not know what that war was about, and didn't give a shit anyway. Instead, he said, "There's coffee in the pot and meat laid out over there. Help yourselves to 'em."

"Now that's real neighborly of you, Mr. Moss. Thankee kindly." Howard motioned to his brothers, and they hurriedly grabbed cups from inside the driving boxes of their wagons and stepped nice and lively to the coffeepot.

Blood at Bear Lake

Howard looked to be the oldest of the brothers, perhaps as old as Joe, while Tom and Benjamin would be in their late twenties or early thirties. All were dressed in flannel and homespun and were barefoot. They were lean and shaggy, with unkempt hair and dark, uncut beards. They seemed to be unarmed save for the large knives on their belts.

If they had no rifle to hunt with, that could explain the way they pounced on the antelope carcass, each man carving away a huge chunk of meat to roast. If they kept at it that way, Joe thought, it would all be gone before daybreak.

Not that he gave a damn. He had given it all. They were welcome to use it when and how they pleased.

Joe turned away from the grunting and gasping as the three men gorged themselves, barely taking time to sear the outside of the slab of meat before they gulped it down, blood running into their beards.

He turned away, intending to step a few paces off and drop his britches to crap, but stopped short when he saw movement inside the second wagon.

The end canvas fluttered, then was drawn back a few inches and an eye appeared, peeping out from behind the filthy canvas.

"Who're you?" Joe asked.

"Don't be paying her no mind," a voice behind him said. There was an edge of challenge in the tone, Joe thought. A cold edge of warning.

Joe grunted. Like he himself said a few moments earlier, none of this was any of his nevermind.

But he changed direction and walked farther from the wagons before he squatted.

✛ 22 ✛

JOE SAT CROSS-LEGGED just outside the circle of firelight, smoking his pipe and listening to the belches, farts,
and occasional words that came from the Wickersham brothers. They had gorged themselves on antelope meat and
now were sharing a jug back and forth among themselves.
Whiskey no doubt. They did not offer to share any with Joe.

He noticed that they had not taken any food to the
woman in the wagon. Or women. There could be more than
one in there for all he knew. He got the impression, though,
that however many there were, they would have to scavenge the leavings of the men if they wanted food.

Joe was tempted to carry something to the wagon. A
slab of meat or a few twists of stick bread. But the brothers
were sure to resent that and rightfully so. It was not his
place to mix into their family matters regardless of what
that might entail.

By the time the brothers were done eating, it was fully

dark, the night cool and the canopy of stars burning bright. One of them said something and the other two laughed. Howard raised his voice and called, "Woman. Come out here."

Which suggested there was only one woman inside the wagon. It was about time they let her eat, Joe thought.

There was movement behind the canvas, and almost immediately a dark form dropped over the tailgate of the wagon and came slowly toward the fire.

"Don't you dawdle, damn you, or you'll get y'self another whuppin'," Howard snapped.

The woman increased her pace. A little. It was obvious that she was reluctant to come, although she surely would be hungry at this hour. Unless she had food in the wagon. She could have been in there nibbling hardtack all day and be stuffed as full as a Christmas goose for all he knew.

When she reached the light and he got a look at her, he was surprised. She was young. Probably no more than twenty if she was that old. And she was pretty. She was small, not standing much more than five feet tall. She had dark hair worn in a tidy bun. She was barefoot, but must have been accustomed to going without shoes because she did not hop or grimace or complain when she walked across the sharp stones and gravel of the soil here.

Did not grimace. Did not, in fact, show any expression that Joe could perceive. She was as solemn and stony-faced as a riverboat gambler. She walked near to the fire and stopped, head down, making no move toward a chunk of meat that lay on a slab of rock beside the fire nor toward the coffeepot that sat close to it.

"The boys and me is thirsty," Howard told her.

The girl looked not at the brothers but at Joe. For the first time, she exhibited a facial expression. She closed her eyes and began to cry, tears welling up under her lashes and rolling down her cheeks. The tears caught the firelight and looked like bright jewels that reached the corners of her mouth and disappeared there.

"Don't just stand there, damn you. Open up."

Still crying, still with her eyes tight shut, the woman reached with trembling fingers to reluctantly unfasten the row of buttons at her throat and down the front of her dress.

She spread the dress open, exposing pale, meaty breasts with huge, engorged nipples.

Tom Wickersham snorted and yelled, "Me first, Howard. You promised. Me first."

"Well, go ahead, boy. Don't keep us'uns waiting."

Tom stood before the woman and fondled her left breast for a moment. Then he bent down, took her nipple into his mouth, and began to suckle, snorting and slurping like a pig suckling its dam.

Joe's first thought was that Tom's beard must have tickled, but if it did she did not show it. She did not show much of anything, but a flush of embarrassment darkened her face and throat as she stood there being humiliated in front of a complete stranger.

While Thomas was bent over sucking milk from the woman, Benjamin stood with a grin and approached her, crouching down to position himself for a drink from the other side.

"Hold it," Howard snapped before Benjamin had a chance to suck on the woman's other tit. "I want me some milk for my coffee." He cackled loudly, grabbed a coffee cup, and stepped across the fire to reach the others.

Howard grasped the woman's tit while Thomas continued to root and snort at the other one. He squeezed hard enough to turn the flesh around his fingers white. The woman rose onto tiptoes and winced at the pain, but she did not cry out nor did she try to pull away from the pain. Howard held his cup beneath her nipple and caught a stream of white fluid squirting out of her body. After a moment, Howard turned away and nodded to Benjamin. "All right, boy. You c'n take what's left."

"How 'bout him?" Benjamin asked, glancing toward Joe.

"What d'ya mean? What about him?"

"Do you want t' offer him a drink o' milk, too, Howard? Old Tessa might like the look o' him, eh? She might like havin' somebody else pull at her dugs."

"I don't give a shit what she'd like," Howard snarled. Then he grinned. "But y' know, it mightn't be such a bad notion after all. Teach her a thing or two, eh?" He laughed and turned toward Joe. "Hey, you, whatever your damn name is. You want t' have you a drink when the boys is done with her? Seems the least we'uns can do after you give us this meat an' coffee an' them fine horses an' all."

"I'm not thirsty, thanks. And I don't recall giving you any horses," Joe said.

"You don't?" Howard acted surprised. Then he chuckled and snapped his fingers. "By damn, that's right. You didn't. But you's going to, ain't you?" He reached around behind him and motioned to the others with a wave of his hand.

Benjamin pushed the woman away and stood upright. He and Thomas both turned to face Joe. The brothers spread a few paces apart, the two younger ones flanking Howard.

All three of the Wickershams drew their knives. They displayed the confidence of superior numbers. Three against one.

"I ast you a question, mister. You's gonna give us them horses now, ain't you?"

81

Gary Franklin

Joe did not know what sort of reaction they expected from him. Fear, probably, at the odds, fear at the sight of those deadly knives.

"Well?"

Joe grinned back at the eldest Wickersham.

✦ 23 ✦

"THEY'S NO PLACE for you to run, mister, so whyn't you give it up? We won't hurt you none. Just take that fine-lookin' horse and the mule. Take them an' whatever else you got." He laughed. "But we won't touch a hair on your old gray head."

Joe frowned. "Am I really starting to get some gray in my hair?"

Howard Wickersham looked puzzled. "Why in the hell are you worried 'bout your damned hair turnin' gray when there's three of us standin' here ready t' cut your gizzard out? An' don't think about pulling that pistol gun an' scaring us away. We don't scare. An' I got to warn you, mister. Do you go an' hurt any one of us, the other two'll cut you up to bite-size chunks for the buzzards."

"No, seriously," Joe said, "am I starting to go gray-headed?"

"Damn you, mister, you ain't takin' us serious."

Joe shrugged. "Why should I worry about a bunch of dead men?"

"Where do you find any dea—*what*?" Howard turned to his brothers and shouted, "Get him, boys. Cut him good."

Thomas started circling around Joe in one direction, Benjamin in the other. Joe suspected that their plan—one they must have used before with a successful outcome—was for the three of them to trap him in the center of a triangle so that his back had to be toward at least one of them at all times.

It was a perfectly good plan, he conceded. If he allowed them to carry it out.

"I bet you boys never faced one o' these," Joe said as he pulled his Colt revolver out of his sash.

"Hey now—!" Howard yelped, his expression indignant. But then perhaps he considered it unfair for someone to fight back against the three of them.

Joe cocked the Colt.

"We was just—"

Joe triggered a ball into Howard's face, whirled, and dropped to his knee.

He pointed the revolver without aiming and fired again, this time at Benjamin, who was standing still, obviously shocked by the blood that was streaming down Howard's face and soaking into his beard.

Joe's bullet hit Benjamin in the chest. Benjamin dropped his knife and sank to his knees, but Joe did not see. He was already turning back toward Thomas, who was now charging forward with his knife extended, expecting to stick Joe in the back.

Joe threw himself down, somersaulting underneath Thomas's blade and coming to his feet beside the wiry younger man. He did not take time to cock the revolver or to reach for his own knife or tomahawk, but lashed out with the Colt. The barrel slashed across Thomas's face, the raised front sight cutting on top of his eyes.

Thomas cried out and tried to cut Joe, but Joe darted back from the sweeping blade, then stepped forward and again struck with the barrel of his revolver, this time smashing down on Thomas's wrist.

Thomas's knife fell from suddenly nerveless fingers and the dark-bearded killer stood there defenseless.

"Quarter," Thomas cried quickly, spreading his hands wide and dropping to his knees. "I claim quarter."

"What the hell d'you mean 'quarter'?" Joe said.

"That means you can't hurt me. You gotta take me prisoner, mister."

"I don't want no damn prisoners," Joe told him.

"No, mister, that's the rule. Does a man claim quarter, you's gotta give it to him."

"Where'd you learn such silly shit as that?" Joe asked, genuinely curious now.

"All my life I knowed it. Me an' all my fam'bly back home in the mountains. It's the rule, mister."

"Well, I ain't from your mountains," Joe said calmly.

"Mister, I a'tellin' you, I'm claiming quarter."

"And if I don't wanta give quarter, just what are you gonna do about it?" Joe glanced over at Benjamin, who was flopping around on the ground with a bullet in his chest, then at Howard, who sat cross-legged with his head down and his hands in his lap, blood turning his beard red and dripping onto his belly.

"Quarter, mister," Thomas shouted, "quarter." He was beginning to sound frantic. And annoying.

"I'll give you quarter, you son of a bitch."

"Oh, thank—"

Joe cocked the revolver and fired point-blank into

Thomas's left temple. The youngest Wickersham went down face-first onto the gravel and did not even bounce when he hit the ground.

"Piece o' shit," Joe muttered as he walked over and stood beside Benjamin.

"I'm shot," Benjamin whined. "Help me. I'm shot."

"Yes, you are," Joe agreed. "Twice." He took careful aim and shot Benjamin between the eyes.

He looked across the clearing to Howard, who had raised his chin and was looking at Joe with dull, almost disinterested eyes. "Don't . . . don't shoot me, mister. I'm beggin' you."

"All right," Joe said as he stepped over to Howard's side.

"You mean that, mister? You ain't gonna shoot me like you done my brothers?"

"I mean it."

"Thank you. Thank you, I . . . *Jesus God!*" he screamed when he saw the bowie in Joe's hand.

Joe lifted Howard's beard out of the way and sliced the man's throat clear through his windpipe. A mixture of air and blood gurgled briefly in the suddenly opened throat; then Howard was still.

Joe grunted softly, then began reloading the fired chambers in his revolver. Handy damn things these revolvers, he reflected. He could have used one a time or two back in the old days.

He looked toward the wagon where the woman had scampered as soon as she saw what the brothers were up to.

✛ 24 ✛

"Y OU CAN COME out now," Joe said softly when he was done dragging the bodies off into the brush and kicking some dirt over the blood that was soaking into thirsty soil. "I ain't gonna hurt you."

He hunkered down beside what was left of the fire and reached for the coffeepot. He was on his second cup when the woman's tear-streaked face finally appeared beneath the canvas wagon top.

"Are you hungry?"

Her only answer was a hesitant nod.

Joe stood, his knee cartilage cracking loudly, and walked over to the antelope carcass, where he sliced off a goodly chunk and carried it back to the fire. He replenished the coals to get a good flame to sear the outside of the meat and keep the juices in where they belonged, then laid the meat onto a flat rock that he shoved into the fire. The aroma of roasting meat quickly spread through the clearing where he had made his camp.

"Supper's ready," he said a few minutes later. "Come and get it."

He was not entirely sure the woman would risk coming near, but if she did not, that was her choice and she was entitled to it. If she could not figure out that he meant her no harm, then piss on her.

After a few more minutes, though, her face appeared again, this time at the front of the wagon. She peered out, then carefully climbed over the back of the seat and down to the ground. Joe remained by the fire.

"Can I . . . I mean . . ." She stood beside the fire, nervous and poised to flee should he make any sudden move.

Joe motioned toward the piece of cooked antelope. "It's yours. I already had what I wanted of it."

"Oh, I . . . thank you." She fluffed her skirts out and settled on the opposite side of the fire. At some point since she ran back to the wagon, she had properly buttoned her dress and combed her hair, too. She looked much better now. Joe suspected she had deliberately presented herself as unattractively as possible in order to minimize the brothers' interest in her. If so, it hadn't worked, but she looked much nicer now that her hair was combed. A proper brushing would positively make it shine, he thought. Not like Fiona's of course, but . . . He felt himself growing hard. It was not a reaction he wanted, but a man's body and his heart do not always travel in the same direction.

Joe cleared his throat abruptly and introduced himself. "What's your name, ma'am?"

"Brenda Coyle," she said softly.

Joe raised an eyebrow. "I kinda thought you was married to one o' them Wickershams."

"Lord, no," the young woman said with considerable

feeling. "I'd as leave marry a snake as one of them. I am . . . I mean I was . . . their slave. My husband and our baby girl was taken by influenza when we was trying to reach California. The Wickershams took me in. As a Christian charity, they said. Then they split off away from the train where I had friends who would have protected me.

"They made me . . . I don't want to talk about the things they did, but they made me their slave. You saw . . ." Her complexion darkened as she remembered how much this stranger had already seen. "You saw what they did this evening. They did much worse than that along the way."

"That's all over now," Joe said. He stood. "I expect the stuff in these wagons belongs to you now. You can do whatever you want about them, but was I in your shoes, I reckon I'd put all them animals into one hitch, throw out most o' the load on that one wagon, an' travel on without the rest of it."

"That wagon . . . that one there . . . was my husband's and mine. It is better, I think, than theirs."

"All right. Do you know how to rig the hitch an' drive them?"

"I think so."

"Well, if you don't now, you damn soon will," Joe told her.

"With your help," she said.

Joe shook his head. "Something you'd best understand, Miz Coyle. You're headed for Colorado. I'm going t'other way. To Wyoming. I can't take the time to guide you west. And anyway, both you an' them animals need a chance to rest up and prepare yourselves for what lies ahead.

"If you think the worst part of the journey is over, ma'am, that's because you ain't yet seen the Sierras. An' I can't be taking the time to guide you. Make that clear in your mind, please."

Gary Franklin

"But you can't just leave me out here by myself."

"No, I won't do that. There's a Mormon settlement not too awful far ahead. You'd be safe there. I figure to take you to them . . . it won't be all that far off my way . . . and leave you there.

"Now, if you will excuse me, ma'am, I'd like to lay down and get some sleep tonight."

"You have been very helpful, Mister . . . Moss, was it?"

"Yes, ma'am. Joseph Moss I be."

"Thank you," she said around a mouthful of antelope.

She was pretty, Joe thought. Even with grease running down her chin. "Good night."

✛ 25 ✛

JOE WOKE SUDDENLY, his senses alerted to danger. Something in the night sounds was not right. He had no conscious recollection of whatever it was that roused him, but a lifetime spent living with danger kept him from doubting the need for caution.

Anyone observing him would not have been able to tell that he had wakened. His eyes remained closed and his breathing slow. But his hand tightened a little on the haft of the tomahawk that he slept with. And he focused all his attention on the sounds that surrounded him.

The soughing of the breeze and the flutter of a bird's wing were ignored. The soft, muted crunch of gravel underfoot was not.

Someone was very stealthily approaching from the other side of the dying fire.

Joe allowed his eyes to open a little. Not fully enough to

91

reflect any lingering firelight, but enough to let him see just a little in the direction of those soft noises.

It was Mrs. Coyle. She was—he had to look again to make sure of it—completely naked. She had nothing in her hands. No gun or knife or any other object that he could see. She was bent over low to the ground and was placing her feet with great care, as if intending total silence.

Perhaps this was some sort of religious rite he had never heard of, he guessed. Or she could have been driven mad by the experience with the Wickershams. Might even have been mad before her capture and imprisonment.

For that matter, Joe had only her side of that story. It could be that she herself killed her husband. Their child, too. Joe had heard of such things among pioneering women who could not adapt to the hardships and the loneliness of life on the fringes of civilization. Brenda Coyle could well be one of those.

Come to think of it, he realized, he could not even be certain that her name indeed was Brenda Coyle. One of the Wickersham boys, he could not remember which one, re-ferred to her as Tessa. Her true name could be either of those. Or neither.

Joe waited. Wondering. Feigning sleep.

The naked woman paused for a moment and stood poised in a low crouch, her tits dangling heavy and full. She took a deep breath and lowered herself to her hands and knees.

She did not stop again until she was kneeling beside Joe's blankets.

She reached forward and took hold of his blanket. Very slowly, she peeled it back, laying it open. Again she paused.

Then she began unfastening the buttons of his fly.

Why the hell was she trying to open his britches? Did she think he carried his money in a pouch there? Damn!

Blood at Bear Lake

Joe did not for a moment believe he was in any danger from this unarmed five-foot-tall female. He decided to wait a little longer before acknowledging that he was awake.

He let her unbutton his fly and spread his trousers open.

Then—he could scarcely believe it—Mrs. Coyle bent down low. He could feel the warmth of her breath on him there. And she took his softly into the warmth of her mouth.

"Hey!"

His unexpected shout in the silence of the night startled the woman so badly that she screamed and fell backward.

Into the fire.

That made her scream again as she hurriedly rolled off the ash-covered coals.

Joe bounded to his feet and grabbed her by the wrist to help pull her free of the fire. She ended up sitting on the ground with her hair disheveled and a dark smudge of ash covering a burn on her backside. She was bawling and babbling something, the words tumbling out so fast and slurred that he could not make them out.

For his part, Joe's pants, still open, had fallen to knee level when he jumped up. Now he hastily retrieved them and got himself covered again and fully buttoned.

Snorting with disgust—more with himself than with Mrs. Coyle—he added wood to the coals and built the fire up so he would have enough light to spread some soothing grease on Mrs. Coyle's burn.

But while he did that, dammit, he intended to get some answers out of her.

"I just . . . I just wanted to make you *like* me," she blubbered between sobs. "So you would, you know . . . take *care* of me. So you would take me to California."

"I already told you," Joe said, taking another dab of lard out of the bucket and spreading it onto her butt. A too damned nice butt for comfort actually. He was a married man now. That was not necessarily easy to remember. Especially when he was rubbing grease over that tight and shapely ass. "Already told you, California ain't the direction I'm headed. I got serious business back in Wyoming country."

"I would be good to you, Joe. I would dress nice for you and fix myself up real pretty. I would do anything you want, Joe." She lowered her voice almost to a whisper. "*Anything.*"

"Dammit, stop tryin' to tempt me." He sat back from where she lay facedown on his blankets. He grabbed a handful of wiry grass and pulled it free of the soil, then used the grass to wipe his hands.

Mrs. Coyle rolled over, ignoring whatever pain that must have cost her and likely smearing lard onto his blanket, too. She was still naked, her breasts hanging free. He could see droplets of milk gathering on the tips of her nipples and gleaming in the firelight. An errant but insistent thought made him wonder what that milk would taste like. "I would be so very, very good to you, Joe. Truly I would. Don't you want me, Joe? You are looking at me here. Would you like to have some of this?" She lifted her right breast on the palm of her hand and leaned forward as if holding it out to him. "I'm a good milker. My baby was fat and healthy on my milk."

Joe ignored the offer. Or tried to. "Why should I believe anything you tell me? You lied to me already."

She scowled. "I never," she said indignantly.

"Woman, I don't even know your right name."

"I told you that. My name is Brenda Coyle. My husband was Jonathan Coyle from Warfordsburg, Pennsylvania. My baby was Abraham Coyle. We named him in honor of President Lincoln. Our home was . . ."

Blood at Bear Lake

"Why'd the Wickershams call you Tessa?" Joe interrupted.

"That one boy, Thomas, he called me that. It was a big joke to the three of them. Their family used to own a nigra slave called Tessa. They said she was fat and ugly but she made good milk and was the nursemaid to any young'uns on the farm. Orphaned animals, too, sometimes. They said they used to sneak over to the slave shack sometimes and get milk from her, too. They said their daddy would beat them black and blue whenever he caught them, but they would go back again anyway. They said woman's milk is way better than cow's milk. Do you think so, Joe? Would you like some of my . . ."

"Shut up!" Joe snapped. "An' go cover yourself. I done told you. I'm a married man."

"But I . . ."

"Go. Right now, dammit, or I'll give you a worse beating than the Wickershams ever thought of."

Sighing heavily, she stood, gave him one more look, then went back to her wagon and climbed into it for the night.

Joe lay down again.

But he had a terrible time getting to sleep that night.

✦ 26 ✦

EXCEPT FOR THE lack of sex—and he could have gotten that from her, too, simply for the asking—having Brenda Coyle in camp was very much like having an Indian woman, which he had done every winter for years and years back in his fur-trapping days.

Brenda rose early and worked like a dog building up the fire, making coffee, scavenging wood, frying meat, and watering the livestock. Joe figured she intended to be on her best behavior with him now. He had refused her offer of sex to make herself wanted in his camp, so now she was trying to ingratiate herself with him as a camp swamper.

Joe smiled to himself as he hunkered beside the coals with a last cup of coffee. This helpfulness was something that was not going to sway him . . . but she was damn sure welcome to keep it up. Just as long and as much as she cared to.

He could not help thinking just a little wistfully that it

was a fearsome shame he could not take her up on her first offer. She was a mighty fine-looking woman.

He couldn't help thinking, too, that he really would have liked a chance to try some of that milk that was dripping out of her and wetting the front of her dress this morning. Her teats were full to overflowing now with no one to take the milk from her.

He wondered if . . . just as a charitable sort of thing . . . He shook his head. No, dammit. Best put *that* sort of thought well aside.

"Would you like more coffee, Mr. Moss?"

"No, thank you, Mrs. Coyle. This is enough for me." He glanced toward the east, where a bright red sliver of sun had begun to appear on the horizon. "It's getting late."

He stood, tossed the last of his coffee onto the coals, and handed her the empty cup. "If you will excuse me, ma'am, I'll get the animals hitched. Are you sure you won't change your mind about that lead wagon, ma'am? Might be some valuable things in there, things you could sell when you get wherever 'tis you're going."

"No, Mr. Moss. I already told you. I want none of their possessions. They were evil men and they did me wrong, but even so, I won't profit from their deaths. Thank you, though."

"You wouldn't mind if I paw through there, then?"

"Do whatever you wish, sir. The wagon is yours. I certainly don't want it. Besides, you've already made it clear you don't want me, so I got nothing to say about what you do. I got no claim upon you."

"Very well. Then if you'll excuse me . . ." Joe touched the brim of his hat and left the breaking of camp to her.

He had been waiting for daylight so he could see while he rummaged through the contents of the wagon that had belonged to the Wickershams. Brenda wanted her own things in her own wagon, the one she and her husband had started west with, but nothing that had been property of her captors.

Joe had already emptied the pockets of the three dead men. He did that when he disposed of their bodies the evening before. He did not consider the act to be any sort of robbery, but a matter of simple practicality. Leaving perfectly good cash money lying there for the vultures and the coyotes to scatter would have been foolish. Not that the Wickershams had had so very much in their pockets when they died. He had taken thirty-some dollars in coin from them and another twenty or thereabouts in currency. All of it rested now in the pouch at Joe's belt.

And he had it in mind that those three brothers would not have set out for California with less than a hundred dollars in hand. Somewhere inside that wagon was their stash, and again it would have been sheer foolishness to leave it for some future traveler to find.

He crawled inside the overloaded wagon and, ignoring the stink of other men's sweat, began swiftly examining things, and then when he was done with each item, tossing it out over the tailgate.

"Mr. Moss, what are you doing in there? I thought you wanted to get on the road today. Why, it'll take me half the morning just to get this all packed back where it belongs."

"I thought you said you didn't want none o' this crap, Mrs. Coyle."

"That's right, I don't."

"Well, I don't neither an' it's in my way."

"Oh, it does seem a shame to let such a nice teapot go to waste. It's silver, I do believe."

"It's yours, ma'am. Figure it's a gift from me t' you."

"Why, I . . . thank you, Mr. Moss."

"My pleasure, Miz Coyle." Joe continued with his task,

throwing out each piece one by one, clothing, furniture, and all.

He salvaged all of the coffee and bacon the Wickershams had been carrying, and some of their lard and flour. Mrs. Coyle took the rest of those along with the silver teapot.

Still, Joe kept looking.

He finally found what he had been searching for contained in a cloth bag tacked to the back of a drawer in a little chest that held harness-making tools.

Joe did not take time to count the coins in the bag, but it was satisfyingly heavy and all the coins were gold. He did not see any silver when he looked into the poke. At a guess, there should be more than a thousand dollars in gold there, perhaps considerably more.

"We can hitch up an' go now," he said as he climbed back out of the wagon.

"What about all of . . . this?" She pointed to the jumble of goods he had thrown out of the wagon. "Do you want me to put it back?"

"Why? I ain't takin' it. You said you don't want it neither."

"But . . ."

"Miz Coyle, the livestock that's left to you an' the brothers are in bad shape. If they was healthy, it'd be all they can do t' pull one wagon, never mind two. So I figure t' build the strangest damned . . . excuse my language, ma'am . . . strangest dang mixed hitch anybody ever seen. But I'm thinkin' with all of 'em pulling your one wagon, we can get you back to a little Mormon settlement that I seen the last time I was through here."

He grinned. "Didn't pay much attention to it then, bein' as how them Mormons don't much hold with carousing an' I wasn't yet a married man at the time. But I figure you can settle there long enough t' get rested an' wait for a train t' pass through so's you can get on to California." The grin became wider. "Or get you a husband if you don't mind becoming a Mormon."

"I don't know what the Mormons hold with, Mr. Moss."

"Don't you worry about that. Fifteen minutes after we get there, you will have been told all about it. An' fifteen minutes after that, you will've been baptized Mormon if you're willin'. Now, if you'll excuse me, I reckon that wagon sheet will make a good cover for the packs on my mule an' I think I'm gonna take it." Joe turned and began untying the white canvas sheet that covered the bows over the bed of the Wickershams' wagon.

✥ 27 ✥

THE FARTHER EAST they went, ever closer to the Green River that he remembered so fondly from the fur-trapping days of his youth, the closer they got to Paiute country. In the old days, he and the boys referred to the Paiutes as Digger Indians.

The Diggers were known as the poorest of all the tribes. Man, woman, or child, they went naked except for the dust and filth that covered them. The problem with the Diggers was that while they were still poor, sometime in the last twenty years or so the bastards had gotten some firearms in hand, most of them stolen from the many wagons that passed through on their way to California.

It turned out that the Diggers were mean and sneaky sons of bitches once they had better weapons than the sticks they used to hunt with. Nowadays, they thought it grand sport to rob and kill any white men they could lull into inattentiveness with their begging and bowing.

Joe knew that, knew it good and well, and there was no way he would have let a pack of Diggers close to his odd little caravan of one wagon and a pack mule.

He was, dammit, lulled into inattentiveness, though. Not by any display of innocence staged by the Diggers. He became complacent because on the eighth day, swinging south of the salt desert and inland salt sea, they finally reached civilization.

Almost.

They were within three miles of the Mormon settlement, he judged, Joe riding well out in front of Mrs. Coyle and her plodding oxen, and he could as good as taste the fresh meat and fruit pies he fully intended to indulge in once they got there. One more ridge to cross, maybe two, and they would be there.

His mouth was watering in anticipation of the fried chicken and oven-baked biscuits he knew would be available in the settlement. It was all he could do to keep from trying to hurry the wagon along. He would have, too, had Mrs. Coyle's animals been in better shape.

As it was, they were in bad need of some decent feed and a long rest. One ox in particular worried him. He suspected the animal might never recover from what it had been through, and probably should be butchered. It would be too tough for steak, but would still be useful for stew meat or for jerky.

Steaks. Beef sizzling over the fire. Thick and juicy slabs of red meat that . . .

Joe was shaken out of his reverie by an ear-shattering whoop from his right and another from the far side of Brenda Coyle's wagon.

Half a dozen arrows rose out of the scrubby brush that a civilized man would not think thick enough to hide a jackrabbit, much less a fully grown Digger Indian.

Blood at Bear Lake

At least one arrow hit one of Mrs. Coyle's oxen—naturally, the one hit was one of the healthier animals, Joe immediately grumbled to himself—and the beast jerked its head, rolling its eyes and bawling in pain.

The ox stumbled and went to its knees, nailing the wagon in place, with no possibility that Mrs. Coyle might be able to run away from the ambush.

Joe was not so encumbered. He was riding his horse, the mule being tethered to the tailgate of the wagon.

He was free to run, which under normal circumstances would have been the sensible thing to do.

But, dammit, he could not throw the spurs to the Palouse and leave a defenseless woman behind for the Diggers to rape and murder, sensible or not.

He snatched the head of the Palouse around and raced back to the wagon, pulling the Spencer carbine from its saddle boot as he did so.

✢ 28 ✢

JOE HEARD THE Palouse grunt. A moment later, it went to its knees from a full run, spilling him over its head. He hit the ground rolling and came up onto hands and knees, somehow still clinging to the Spencer that was locked in his grip.

Scuttling like a crab—like one damned quick-moving crab—he scrambled the remaining distance to the heavy wagon.

"Fall back, Brenda. Throw yourself over the seat into the wagon bed and hunker down out of the way of them arrows," he shouted, rising into a crouch beneath the wagon box.

Another flight of arrows fluttered toward the halted wagon, half of them burying themselves in the flesh of the terrified oxen, which were bawling and kicking and trying to escape the madness and the copper stink of fresh blood.

Joe had no target to aim at, but he was no tenderfoot. He had fought Indians more than a few times in the past, and he was not about to waste his ammunition cutting brush or raising dust.

A high-arcing arrow hit the iron rim of the wheel Joe knelt beside and skittered off it. It wound up standing upright in the ground by his right foot.

"You sons o' bitches are gonna piss me off if you keep this up," he snarled aloud to no one in particular.

"Did you say something, Mr. Moss?"

He looked up to see Brenda Coyle leaning over the side of the wagon. "Not to you, I didn't. Now get back inside there outa the way," he snapped, motioning her down.

She withdrew, and Joe returned his attention to the Diggers.

He saw a flicker of movement, and the Spencer carbine came swiftly to his shoulder. He took aim and pressed the trigger and . . . and nothing happened. He had forgotten that unlike his Henry, the Spencer had to be cocked in a separate motion after the cartridge was fed into place by the lever.

"Dammit!"

He thumbed the heavy hammer back, but by then he was much too late to try a shot at the spot where he had seen the movement.

More arrows rose lazily upward, rising slowly, then taking a downward turn and falling with increasing velocity until they landed like huge raindrops onto the wagon and the dying, screaming oxen.

The wagon jerked forward, rocked back, jerked again as the oxen struggled to tear themselves free from their torment.

Joe pitied the big, stolid brutes, but there was nothing he could do to help or to protect them. They already looked like pincushions, with arrow shafts protruding at crazy angles from the doomed beasts' backs and hips and sides.

They slung their heads from side to side, sending ropes of bloody foam and snot through the air.

And one by one they went to their knees, rolled onto their sides, and were gone.

The Diggers whooped and danced. Victorious and jubilant now.

Now Joe could see the Indians clearly. They were scrawny, wizened little sons of bitches who probably never had their bellies full in their entire lives, and now they could see several tons of fresh meat lying there in front of them, ready to carve and to cook.

Joe smiled grimly and held his fire.

He had seven cartridges in the Spencer and six balls in his Colt revolving pistol.

And when those were gone, he would still have his bowie knife and his faithful tomahawk.

There were—he tried to count—something like seven Diggers dancing around out there.

In a few minutes, they would grow bold and swarm in to claim their booty and to turn the oxen into meat. After all, the last they had seen of him was when the Palouse went down and he was thrown over its head.

Joe remained hunkered down beside the wagon wheel. Waiting patiently.

When all of the Diggers were in plain sight—three of them coming toward the wagon while four others stayed back covering them with their bows—when Joe was fairly sure he had them exactly where he wanted them, he stood up and carefully, methodically, one target at a time, began slaughtering them.

✠ 29 ✠

JOE DECIDED HE must be getting old. Well, maybe starting to get old. He had a slight twinge low in his back after bending down and taking the scalps from the first five of his seven victims.

He tucked away this last hank of black, greasy hair with the bit of bloody skin attached and stood, bending backward just a little to help ease the muscles in his back.

Joe did not need the scalps of his vanquished foes as trophies, but he continued the practice he had followed for years after first learning it from Indians. According to their belief, at least the way he was given to understand it, a spirit could not join his dead tribesmen in the afterworld if his scalp was taken in this world. A man became truly dead if he gave up his scalp to an enemy. Joe did not know how true any of that was, but he did not intend to take any chances.

He took a moment to rest his back, then stepped over the body of the scalpless Digger Indian and walked over to the next. This one, an emaciated youngster who could not have been more than sixteen or seventeen, was still breathing.

The boy had a hole high in the chest. Bloody froth bubbled on the surface, suggesting he was shot through the lung. It was possible, just barely possible, that someone could recover from a wound like that. Joe had seen it happen.

But not this time.

Joe leaned down and took a grip on the kid's hair to lift his upper body off the ground, then made two quick swipes with the bowie. The first slashed the boy's throat completely through to the bone. The second added another scalp to Joe's collection.

Bastards thought they were going to kill him, did they? Well, he had another thought for them.

Joe finished collecting the last scalp and walked back to the wagon to retrieve his Spencer carbine. He pulled the magazine tube out and dropped in seven fresh cartridges, then set the Spencer aside, reminding himself to get more from his pack. The pack and mule seemed to have survived the attack without harm at the back of the wagon. All the arrows had been directed forward, where the people and oxen were.

"Miz Coyle. You can come out now. It's safe. All the Injuns is accounted for."

Sighing, he walked over to the fallen Palouse horse. That animal had been the best horse he ever owned. Oh, he tended to think that about any good horse that he got hold of, but this time he really meant it. The Palouse had been getting a little long in the tooth, but—dammit—he liked that horse. And it had been his. He could feel the bile rising in the back of his throat as anger overtook him at the sight of the dead horse.

If there had been any of those Diggers still alive, he would have killed them all over again. Bastards!

There was nothing he could do to change it, though. He

could only accept what was and forget about what might have been.

Joe bent down again and unfastened his cinches, then struggled to pull his saddle free of the carcass.

The Diggers' arrows had killed all the livestock, but he was close enough to the little Mormon settlement that Joe figured he could walk over there to buy a horse and haze some oxen or mules back to drag the wagon the rest of the way in. He had to get the saddle off now, though, before the dead horse began to bloat and it became impossible to remove it without cutting the cinches.

"Mrs. Coyle," he called again. "Everything is all right. You can climb down here, Miz Coyle. Be a good idea for you t' do that. I have t' walk over to that town to get fresh animals, and I wouldn't want t' leave you alone out here. There might be some more Injuns nearby. I wouldn't want t' leave you undefended while I go for the animals."

He waited a moment, but heard nothing from inside the wagon.

Joe set the saddle down and quickly stripped the bridle from the horse. Damn shame, though. That had been a mighty fine animal.

"Miz Coyle. Are you all right, ma'am?"

Joe stepped onto a wheel spoke and from that into the driving box. As he did so, he was thinking what a hell of a time he would have trying to wrestle the yokes and riggings from those dead oxen. Possibly, he should bring someone from town to help him with that.

Mrs. Coyle was crouched on the floor of her wagon, wedged in between some crates and boxes.

"Mrs. Coyle? Ma'am?"

Joe crawled over the back of the seat and slipped beneath the canvas wagon sheet. It took a moment for his vision to adjust to the dim light beneath the canvas.

"Aw . . . shit!"

An arrow, one of the many fired high in the air, had plunged downward, piercing the flimsy wagon cover and by horrible chance striking Mrs. Coyle in the back of the neck.

The arrow had hit her spine, Joe saw, so the young widow's death must have been instantaneous. He hoped it was also painless for her.

"Well, shit," he said again, then climbed back out of the wagon and down to the ground.

There was no need now to bring help and fresh livestock from the settlement. As far as he was concerned, the people there were welcome to scavenge anything they wanted out of the wagon. He had no interest in any of it.

He would keep the money the Wickershams had been carrying. His intent had been to give that poke to Brenda Coyle when he got her to safety, but that was off the boards now, of course. He had no interest in anything else at this wagon of death, however.

Joe inspected the mule thoroughly, checking it for wounds, but it had not suffered so much as a nick.

He untied it from the tailgate and led it, skittish and unhappy from the smell of so much blood, around to the front so he could set his saddle and bridle on top of the mule's pack. It would ride there well enough until he could walk to town and buy a horse to ride.

Then, the Spencer balanced in one hand and the mule's lead rope in the other, Joe Moss set out for the Mormon settlement south of the vast salt desert.

✥ 30 ✥

B Y THE TIME he reached the settlement, Joe's feet hurt and his mood was black. He kept thinking that if he had done something different, had done things better, somehow Brenda Coyle would still be alive. Never mind that it was simple bad luck that the arrow had found her. Joe felt responsible for the young woman's death.

Mrs. Coyle, he thought, had had a thoroughly shitty life. Perhaps in death, she would be reunited with her husband and baby.

Joe did not know much about that sort of thing, but it was what the padres claimed, wasn't it? Hell, maybe it was true. He hoped so because if it was, she would likely think her whole awful experience worthwhile. He knew he would do anything, suffer any amount, go through . . . whatever . . . if it meant he could be with Fiona and Jessica again. Likely, Mrs. Coyle would feel the same way about it.

He paused at the edge of the little Mormon town and took a look.

"Town" was too grand a word to describe the place. Bunch of chicken coops was closer to the truth.

Out so far from live timber, wood seemed to be in short supply. Buildings were crude shacks made not from lumber but from immature saplings that were planted close together in trenches like tall fences, then roofed with heavy canvas. Most of the canvas looked suspiciously like old wagon covers put to new use.

There were only a handful of buildings, two of which were large enough to suggest they were business establishments of some sort. The others looked like people's homes. None of the buildings had signs posted to indicate what they were.

The structures were all ranged on either side of a single long "block" with privies, pens, and livestock corrals behind.

Since there were no hitch rails provided for passersthrough, Joe tied his mule's lead rope to the horn of his saddle and dropped the saddle in the dirt to act as a hitching anchor, then entered the largest of the buildings. The shade indoors felt good after the sun's heat outside.

The place was indeed a store, a general mercantile judging by the wide range of goods that were stacked here, there, and elsewhere around the dirt floor. He did not see any clerks.

"Hello? Is anyone here?" he called out. No one came, so he tried again, louder this time.

"I heard you the first time," a woman's voice responded from behind a linen curtain that more or less closed off a doorway. "Just hold your horses. I'll be with you in a minute."

Joe grunted, then turned and began inspecting the merchandise. Not that he needed anything at the moment. He had more than enough to get him to Sol's store at Fort

Laramie, especially after he'd taken everything that looked useful out of the Wickersham and Coyle wagons. Joe figured to resupply from Sol if he needed anything more.

Or if Fiona needed or wanted anything. Anything she wanted, Joe wanted her to have. *Anything!*

"Who is . . . oh! A stranger." Joe caught only a glimpse of the woman who was tending the store. She was plump and middle-aged, with her hair straggling out of the bun she wore. She might have been fairly nice-looking if she hadn't also looked like she needed a shave; she had quite a nice mustache, or anyway would have if she took the time to wax it. She also had one side of her dress hiked up, caught underneath the cord that tied her apron in place.

Judging by the woman's bright red complexion, her rapid breathing, and most of all, the sound of heavy boots moving around in the back of the place, Joe kind of thought he had interrupted her at a most inopportune time.

"Sorry t' bother you, ma'am, but I'm needing some help," he said.

"No bother, I was just . . . tidying up in back."

"Uh-huh," Joe said. He tried not to, but the hint of a grin tugged at his lips. He had heard it called a lot of things, but "tidying up" was a first.

Joe coughed into his fist to give himself time to get rid of that grin, then said, "Two things I'm needin', ma'am. First is a stout drink. Second, I need t' buy me a horse. Mine was killed by Injuns just a little ways west from here and . . ."

"Indians!" the woman cried. "Oh, no." She turned around and fled out the back door before Joe had time to say another word.

"Peterson," the big man said, extending his work-hardened hand to Joe. "Aaron Peterson."

Joe introduced himself and explained his problem.

Peterson fingered the salt-and-pepper gray beard that hung down onto his chest, then said, "You got them all?"

"That isn't what I said. I said I got all that I saw. One or two could've got away without me knowing."

"They could bring more of their ugly kind," Peterson said. He sighed. "We were on good terms with the Indians hereabouts," he said. "Now this."

"Could be these Injuns wasn't from around here," Joe suggested. "Could be they was out raiding, lookin' for food. They was all scrawny. Their bellies was sunk in deep. Hell, I woulda give them food if they'd just asked. I been hungry myself a time or two."

Peterson fingered his beard some more, obviously assessing the threat to his own settlement if there were more hostiles in the vicinity.

"Mr. Peterson, where could you an' me set down and have us a drink whilst we ponder on this? I could sure go for a glass o' whiskey now."

"Oh, we have no hard spirits here, Mr. Moss. We are Mormon, you see. We don't drink liquor."

Joe grinned. "I've knowed a lot o' Mormons, Mr. Peterson, and got drunk with some of 'em."

"Not with any man here, you haven't. You won't either. We do not permit it."

"No booze? All right then, how's about a beer?"

"No alcohol of any sort, Mr. Moss."

"Good heavens, no alcohol at all? Whatever d'you boys do fer relaxation?" Then he remembered the rumpled, breathless woman here in the general store when he walked in. "Never mind," he said. "I think I figured it out. If I can't get a drink, then can I buy a horse? Mine got shot back there."

"We would have little to choose from if you intend to

ride astride. Most of our stock are accustomed to harness, not saddle."

"Reckon I can manage if the animal is any kind of tractable."

"Out here . . . so far from the city . . . the cost might be quite steep, you know."

"I ain't got much cash money," Joe said. Then, considering, he added, "But I could offer some boot. I got me a fine Spencer repeating carbine that I could throw into the deal."

The truth was that he was not all that pleased with the Spencer's performance. It did not load as quickly, nor carry as many cartridges, and—most important—did not hit as hard as his beloved Henry.

He was pretty sure he could pick up another Henry at Sol's store, and he could make do with his Colt revolver until then.

"Repeaters are rare, y'know," Joe said. They were not so terribly rare anymore, especially the Spencers, but Peterson might not know that. "An' they're a comfort against Injuns. Look what mine did for me back there."

"Mr. Moss, I think we can come to a meeting of the minds about this. Come along with me while we look over the horses that might be available."

"Why'n't you carry this here Spencer while we do? Just in case we see some of them Diggers," Joe said, handing the carbine to Peterson, that being one of the little tricks a trader soon learned if he wanted to prosper. Put your goods in the hands of the buyer; it helps to make him regard the item as being already his. Makes it that much harder for him to refuse the deal later on.

✦ 31 ✦

"THIS HORSE IS a piece o' walking shit. You know that, don't you?" Joe asked. And this time, it was no trick of the trade he was employing. The horse that was offered to him really was nothing but a self-propelled pile of bones.

"It is a fine animal, Mr. Moss. Besides, it is the only saddle horse we have."

"Good Lord, Mr. Peterson. Put a saddle on that thing an' I figure the weight o' the saddle alone would be enough t' drive it to its knees. If I tried t' mount it, I might as well just take a gun and shoot it 'cause I'd kill it for certain sure."

"Then I cannot help you."

"Well, I need some kinda mount," Joe said.

Peterson fingered his beard and mumbled a little to himself. He looked Joe up and down, then sighed. "Come over here."

The Mormon leader led Joe out of that shed and across the street to another house. There was a stable behind it that held a monster of a horse, the biggest animal—well, the biggest horse anyway—that Joe had ever seen. It was a gleaming jet black everywhere except for a pure white blaze and four white stockings. It must have stood seventeen hands or close to it and weighed upward of a ton.

"They tell me the breed is called a Shire," Peterson said. "It was abandoned by a family traveling to California. They thought this horse had a broken leg, but the problem was only a stone bruise. It still limps now and then, but the leg is sound. The man who left it here said it was broken to saddle. We've no use for anything that big." Peterson rolled his eyes. "You would not believe how much this horse eats, and there just is not much grass around here to cut for feed."

Joe looked at the horse. Its feet were huge. Shoes for it would have to be the size not of plates, but serving platters. Heavy feathering on the lower legs betrayed its dray horse breeding. But he liked the intelligence that showed in the big horse's eyes, and liked the proud way it carried its head.

"Mind if I give 'im a try before I decide anything?"

"Go right ahead."

Joe led the big black around to the street and dropped the lead, figuring if the Shire tried to walk away, Peterson would be there to get it back under control. There was no need for that, however. The Shire stood ground-hitched while Joe went over to the mule and fetched his saddle and bridle.

"The horse is used to a snaffle, not that curb bit," Peterson said. "I doubt your little bit would fit in that big mouth anyway."

"You got a bigger snaffle?"

"Of course. Just a minute." Peterson went into the store, and emerged a moment later carrying a brand-new snaffle bit. He quickly changed it for Joe's bit on the bridle.

The snaffle fit in the Shire's mouth without a problem,

but Joe had to let his bridle out as far as the straps allowed in order to get it properly set on the black's big head.

He found the same problem when he tried to put his saddle in place. The cinch straps on both sides had to be repositioned before he could get the cinch around the Shire's barrel.

Joe looked the horse up and down, then grunted. "If I was half an inch shorter, I'd need a damn stepladder t' get onto him."

"Go ahead, Mr. Moss. Ride him as long as you like. Then you can decide if you want him. But I have to be honest with you. The choice is either this big freak or the old horse across the way there."

"That ain't a horse, Mr. Peterson, it's a sorrow waiting t' happen."

"Then this would be all we have to offer."

"I sure as hell hope he travels well under saddle then, Mr. Peterson."

Joe stepped—climbed would be more accurate—onto the black's back and sat there with his legs spread wide by the sheer size of the Shire. After a moment, he made sure of the reins in his hand, then touched his heels to the black's sides.

✤ 32 ✤

THE SHIRE WAS not fast, but he was hell for stout. Over the next few days, Joe discovered that he simply could not wear the black out. The horse would travel all day and all night, too. It was even tougher than a mule. It had a trot that would rattle a man's teeth, but it could hold a fast walk for hours at a time if that was what was asked of it. By the time he reached the Mormon town of Salt Lake City, Joe had come to quite like the big Shire, even if it did attract a good bit of attention.

The only problem he had was not with the horse but with the saddle. His comfortable Mexican saddle was made to fit on a normal horse, not this huge mountain of horseflesh, and after a very few days of travel, Joe could see that the horse was developing sores despite the blankets Joe used to pad the saddle.

He stopped at a good saddlery in Salt Lake City, run by

a man named Stevens, to take care of that before it might become a serious problem.

"I can do the work for you, mister. I'll have to build a new tree, but I can use the leather you already have here. I will just take your old saddle apart and rebuild it with the wider tree. Can you leave the horse and your saddle here for a couple days?"

"I'm in a hurry," Joe said. "I got to meet up with my wife."

"I understand that, but you won't travel too well if your horse is running blood from saddle sores."

Joe hesitated only for a moment, then nodded. "You're right o' course, but please hurry as much as you can."

"That I will do, sir."

"You have a stable out back?" Joe asked

"We do, yes."

"Then can I leave the mule with you, too? I'll pay for his keep o' course. For the Shire as well."

"Of course."

"And if I'm gonna be here for a while, can you tell me where I can find me a drink in this Mormon town?"

"Well, now, in theory the city is dry. The Church disapproves of liquor, and you are no longer in the United States, you know. The Church pretty much determines the law here in Deseret."

"Yes, sir, I've been told that. I've also been told that a man can find a drink here if he wants one."

Stevens paused for a moment, then lowered his voice almost to a whisper. "Go down here two blocks and turn right. You will find a place called Wilson's Café. They serve something more than coffee there, and the Saints don't come around because they disapprove of coffee, too."

"Thanks." Joe started for the door, then turned back. "One more thing if you don't mind. D'you know a good gun shop around here?"

"Oh, my, yes. There is a very good man who sells guns. That would be back this other way. Just down to the corner and turn left. He has a sign outside. It reads: 'Jonas Whitacker, Gunsmith.' You can't miss it."

"You been a big help t' me, Mr. Stevens. Thanks."

Joe was torn between what he wanted to do and what he really needed to do. And he really needed a long gun. The Spencer simply was not adequate. It did not hit nearly as hard as his old Henry had, and carried only half the number of cartridges.

He put off the pleasure of a glass of whiskey a little longer and headed for Whitacker's gun shop.

Jonas Whitacker proved to be a young man, fat and cheerful. He must have been a good gunsmith, though, because he had a good many firearms in racks waiting to be worked on, each with a tag tied to the trigger guard to indicate who the gun belonged to and what work needed to be done. Most were in for simple things like broken springs.

There was also a shorter rack that held new or nearly new rifles offered for sale. Joe smiled when he saw the familiar brass receiver and telltale lever of a .44-caliber Henry.

"Are you interested in that?" Whitacker asked when Joe picked up the Henry and looked it over. The rifle seemed to be in fine shape, although clearly it had been used.

"Yes, sir, I am. I'm partial to this here model. You got ammunition for it, too?"

"I do."

"Fine. I'll take the rifle then."

"You haven't asked how much I'm asking for it."

"No, but I intend to have this gun. How much?"

"My price is high. Fifty dollars. Back East, that same rifle would cost you twenty dollars at the most."

"We ain't back East, and I ain't quibbling. Not about

this." Joe smiled. "You aren't trying to talk yourself out of a sale here, are you?"

Whitacker laughed. "No. Just trying to be honest with you."

"I like an honest man. An' I'll pay your price. Pay for a couple hundred cartridges, too, if you got them."

"I have them. Two hundred rounds, you say?"

"Aw, make it three hundred. And one of those ramrods there so's I can clean inside the bore proper."

Whitacker nodded. "Excuse me a minute while I get your ammunition. I won't be but a moment."

Joe opened his pouch and plucked out enough gleaming gold coins to pay for his purchases. As soon as Whitacker returned with the boxes of cartridges, Joe opened one and filled the Henry's magazine.

"I don't think you will find anything to shoot in the city here, sir," Whitacker said, obviously disapproving of the idea that anyone would be carrying a loaded rifle in town.

"Mr. Whitacker, I do hope you're right about that." Joe paid the man, then gathered up his purchases and left.

He stopped at Stevens's saddlery long enough to stash his boxes of cartridges and new ramrod with his other things that Stevens was keeping for him.

Then, smiling broadly, he headed for Wilson's Café and that glass of whiskey he had been looking forward to for the past week or more.

✢ 33 ✢

"WELL, I'LL BE a son of a bitch!"

The hairy man in buckskins grinned and said, "Yeah, I heard that about you, Joe."

Joe threw his arms around Cyrus Brainard, tipped his head back, and let rip with a roar that no mountain lion could have matched. "Damn, Cy, what's it been? Four, five years since I seen your ugly face?"

"Som'pin like that."

"All that time"—Joe shook his head—"an' you ain't got a lick handsomer."

"But we's older, Joe. Say, I heard you got killed down in Santa Fe a while back."

"Yeah, but it didn't take. Old Scratch an' me had us one of them duels to see did he get my soul. His mistake was lettin' me choose the weapons, an' I picked knife fighting." Joe laughed. "Only man I ever met could best me in a knife fight, Cy, was you. And I ain't so sure about you."

123

Gary Franklin

"Are you still a drinking man, Joseph?"

"Does a bear shit in the woods?"

"Then let me buy you a drink." Cy winked. " 'Cept here they call it Missouri coffee. Guaranteed to taste like river water. And if they watered it any more, it likely would. Hey, Mike, two Missouri coffee for me and my friend Joe Moss here. Me and him have rode the high mountains together and lifted more scalps than you could tote if you had a wheelbarrow to carry them all in. Hurry up now and don't skimp on the whiskey, hear?"

Joe leaned his new Henry in a corner and took a seat at the table near it. Cy fetched their "Missouri coffee" from the bar and joined him there.

"How's it going for you, Joe?"

"Pretty fair. I got myself hitched for one thing."

"No shit."

"Not no winter marriage neither. I mean the real thing. The forever kind."

"I never would've suspected that from you, Joe. You always had a way with the squaws and the doxies. But permanent? With a decent woman? I never woulda thought it."

"T' tell you the truth, Cyrus, neither would I. How's about you?"

"Oh, a little of this, little of that. I hunted buffalo for a spell. Trapped some wild horses. You know how it is."

"So I do, Cy. But this is a big country. I expect there'll always be a way for the likes of us to scrape by."

Cyrus took a long swallow of the liquor. Which in truth was not all that bad. "Drink up, Joe. Your money ain't no good this evenin'."

"You in the chips now, Cy?"

"I damned sure am. Just got paid off from guiding a fella that thinks he can find a route he can take a railroad across the mountains clear to the Pacific Ocean."

"Then I hope the son of a bitch is wrong because this country would go to hell quick if a railroad ever comes through an' a pile of pork eaters with it."

"I think maybe he can do it, but it wouldn't be easy," Brainard said. "Besides, they're all busy with their war back East."

"That's still going on, is it?"

"Ayuh. It's in all the newspapers."

"I'll have to get me one. A newspaper, I mean."

"Joe, you can't read a damned thing. I seen you make your mark when you sold your plews. You can't even write your own name."

"I can now. I studied on it while I was laid up hurt one time."

Cyrus grinned. "My old friend Joe Moss can read. Now I've heard everything." He finished his whiskey and called for another, then turned back to Joe. "Guess what I'm doing now."

"Hell, Cy, I'd believe most anything. Tell me."

"You know I've hunted just about every beast there is in this country."

"Yeah. We both have."

"Well, now, I've gone to hunting men, too. One man anyway."

"What the hell for?"

"There's a reward out, Joe, for the person who can bring in some crazy sonuvabitch that blew up an entire silver mine back in Nevada. Blew it clean off the map an' killed a bunch of people, too."

"I'll be damned," Joe said. "Who is this fellow?"

"Nobody living seems to know his name, but he got away on a Appaloosa horse." Cyrus accepted his refreshed drink and took a swallow, then cocked his head to one side and half-closed his eyelid on that side of his face. "It occurs to me, Joe, that you used to favor them flashy horses. You still got that old Palouse?"

"No, he got killed. Injun arrow that was intended for me got him instead. He was an awful good horse, though. Now I'm on a big black. Supposed to be a dray horse, but he goes fine under saddle. The more I use him the better I like him, too. Steady as a rock and not stumble-footed like you might think a horse with such big feet would be. Why?"

"I was just asking, Joe, that's all."

Cyrus finished his cup of whiskey, then leaned forward across the table to peer into Joe's eyes. "I won't be able to quit wondering about this, Joe, unless I come right out and ask the question. It will gravel me something awful."

"Then ask it, Cy. You know I won't lie to you, no matter what."

"Joseph, old pard, did you go and blow up a silver mine belonging to a family name of Peabody?"

"Cy, I promised I wouldn't lie to you no matter what you asked, nor will I. Yes. It was me that done it. I had good reason to do it, though. The Peabodys were trying to kill my wife. They still are. You know I won't step back an' let that happen."

"Aw, shit!" Cy pushed his empty cup aside and shifted his chair back a few inches. "Joe, I gave my word an' took money on a deal, too. I promised a man I'd stand watch here in Salt Lake for that man on the Palouse horse."

"And when you found him?" He was sure he already knew the answer to that, but he wanted to make sure before he did anything he might regret later.

"Joe, I took money from the fella . . . a down payment, he called it, to bind the deal . . . you and me is drinking on his money right now."

"What did you promise to do, Cy?"

Blood at Bear Lake

"Dammit, Joe, I promised to kill the fellow for this Peabody."

Joe fingered his chin. Then smiled. "You an' me go back a long way together, so let's at least make this interesting. I've always wondered if I could take you with a knife, Cy. Like I said before, you're the best I ever seen. Except maybe me. Now's our chance to find out which of us is the better hand with a blade."

"Knife only? No tomahawks? You was always way better'n me with a 'hawk, Joseph. It wouldn't be a fair fight was we to use the 'hawks."

"All right, Cyrus. No tomahawks nor pistols neither. Just cold steel, rough an' tumble."

"Like in the old days," Brainard said rather wistfully.

"Yeah, Cy. Like in the old days."

"Then let's have us another drink together before we get down to it. Is that all right with you?"

"Aye, old friend, so it be. But it would please me t' be able to buy the next round of drinks."

"You're a good man, Joe Moss."

"And you're a good friend, Cyrus Brainard."

Joe went to the bar and brought back two more cups of whiskey. He handed one to Cy, saluted him with the cup, and said, "Drink up, friend. At least we can enjoy one last cup together, eh?"

"To old times," Cy said, raising his cup to Joe as well.

"To old times."

"HEY! DAMMIT, LEAVE those tables where I had them," the barman yelled across the room. Joe and Cy were dragging the heavy tables aside to clear a space.

"We won't be long," Cy promised.

"I don't want them moved to begin with," the bartender insisted. "Now put them back where you found them."

"In a minute," Joe told him. "We need us some room here."

"What the hell do you want room for?"

"We're gonna have us a little fight, mountain style."

"A fight! Not in my place you aren't."

"Who's gonna stop us? Some pork eater like you? I don't damn well think so." Cyrus shoved another table to the side and kicked the chairs underneath it to get them out of the way, too.

There were not a great many men in the place, but when they heard there was to be a fight, they crowded close around the rough ring Joe and Cyrus had laid out with the tables and the chairs.

"You boys want a minute to make some bets?" Cy said, laughing. "That's fine if'n you do, but keep one thing in mind. I'm a wild an' woolly he-coon of the mountains. Old Joe here is a fine fella, but his scalp is gonna be on my belt t'night." Cyrus tipped his head back and roared.

"My friend here never figured out that it ain't stew till there's meat in the pot, and he ain't won no fight with me," Joe returned.

"Yet," Cy amended. "And I ain't fixing to neither. Not until you and me has had us one last drink together."

Joe bobbed his head in agreement. "Damn right."

"Barman! Two mugs o' your best. Fill them full to the top, mind you, for one of us is about to have his last drink on this earth."

A buzz swept through the crowd at the news that this would be a fight to the death. Several men ran outside and began shouting the word up and down the street. Then they and a horde of others thundered back inside Wilson's Café.

By the time fresh mugs were delivered, there was barely room enough in the place for another soul to squeeze inside the door, and the bartender was doing a bang-up business. The man was no longer complaining that his tables had been moved, Joe noticed. He was too busy pouring liquor into mugs and money into his cash box to take time for comment for or against the fight.

Joe tossed his whiskey back. Its warm glow spread through his belly, and the effect of the alcohol made him feel loose and ready for anything. He grinned. "You're a good man, Cy. I want you t' know how I feel about that."

"Likewise, Joe. You're a good man and a good friend."

"You ready?"

"Ayuh. Reckon I am." Cy tipped his head back and

drained the last of the liquor from his mug, tiny rivulets of whiskey escaping from either side and running into his beard where it disappeared from sight.

Joe set his empty mug onto the nearest table. Cy tossed his onto the floor.

Cy pulled his knife, a long slender blade that looked like it had started out as an ordinary kitchen butcher knife, but with a handle that had been wrapped in beaded deerskin with long fringes falling from the butt end. Cy had been carrying that same knife for about as long as Joe could remember.

But then the same was true about Joe's old bowie. He drew it out of its sheath now.

Joe smiled at his old friend and nodded.

Words were no longer needed between them.

For the sake of honor, one of them would die here, Cyrus to keep his word to a man whose job he had accepted, or Joe, who would not turn aside from his quest to again find his beloved Fiona.

As one, the two old friends dropped into fighting crouches, free hands slightly extended, knives balanced in their right palms.

As one, they began shuffling slowly to their left. Circling. Watching. Waiting for the other to make that one fatal error.

✦ 35 ✦

A KNIFE FIGHT CONDUCTED between men who know what they are doing looks more like a dance than a brawl. Often, it is decided by a single thrust or slash. But it can take a long time getting to that point.

Each tightening of a muscle or shift of balance can be read by the other. Each time one combatant readies himself to thrust, the other can see and can counter the motion.

Joe knew Cy's fighting style from of old. Cyrus liked to lull an opponent in with a false opening, then lash out and disembowel the other with a cut high on the belly.

Joe himself preferred to bore straight in, battering down the other man's knife hand with a cut across the wrist followed by a stab to the heart. And Cy knew it.

Cy had a slightly longer reach than Joe. Joe felt he was a little the quicker of the pair.

Circling. To the left, always to the left. Right foot forward. Knife held low. Breathing shallow and rapid. No matter how many times a man had done this in the past, it was not something he would ever accept as routine. There was damned sure nothing boring about it. Not to the participants.

The shouting, yammering crowd inside Wilson's Café quickly began to tire of the slow shuffle round and round.

"Come on, you."

"Blood. Show us some blood, eh?"

"Ah, you bastards're jus' playin' around."

"My old granny can fight better'n this."

Joe ignored the fools. Likely, not a single one of them had ever himself been a participant in a knife fight. Cy, however, seemed to flush a little darker as the noise of the hecklers increased and their taunts came from all around the café.

If Cy became thoroughly agitated by the taunts, it would break his concentration and degrade his ability. Joe slowed the pace of his circling. The shouts from the crowd swelled in volume and became nastier.

Joe found that almost comical. How many of these pork eaters would dare to say those things directly to Cyrus or to Joe? They needed the anonymity and the encouragement of a crowd to give them the courage to speak, to say things that they otherwise would not dare lest they get their own scalps lifted.

Very carefully, Joe slowed down even further until he was barely moving.

Cy was breathing rapidly now. His eyes kept cutting back and forth, roving over the shouting faces behind Joe. He was obviously distracted by the crowd.

Joe feigned tripping, but Cy did not take the bait. Joe followed his phony trip with an equally false limp, as if he had pulled a muscle in his left thigh.

And he slowed again, almost coming to a halt, barely moving. To his left. To his left. Circling.

Blood at Bear Lake

The crowd shrieked in fury over the lack of action in this so-called fight to the death they felt had been promised to them.

Joe barely heard, but Cy's face flushed dangerously dark. He had taken just about all he could stand, and Joe knew it.

"Don't do it, old friend," he silently told himself. "Don't."

But Cyrus did.

With a roar he leaped forward, eyes flashing, knife held back until the last possible moment, but then lashing out with all the speed of a striking rattlesnake.

Joe thought he was ready, but even so he misjudged his old friend's ability. He felt an icy cold sensation flick across his left forearm, and knew he had been cut, perhaps badly. Blood began to flow, dripping off his hand.

The crowd roared their approval. There was blood in sight. The volume of their shouts increased until Joe felt he could feel it like a weight pressing in on him from all sides.

Cy grunted, stepped quickly to his right, and his blade flashed again, driving toward Joe's gut.

Joe's own blade darted forward, reaching not to open up Cy's belly, but cutting hard across the hand that held that deadly butcher knife. It was a maneuver that meant Joe's own death if he misjudged the speed or the direction of Cy's thrust. It was all or nothing.

The razor-sharp bowie whipped across Cy's hand.

Cy cried out. He pulled his hand back. Or what remained of it. His thumb, along with his knife, tumbled to the floor. His forefinger had been severed, and dangled loose from what was left of his hand, held there by a thin strip of skin. Cy blanched and ripped it free, letting it drop into the sawdust on the floor.

Cyrus Brainard's knife-fighting days were ended.

But he was still alive. Both of them were.

Joe felt a flush of deep relief.

Cy could snatch up his knife and try to fight with his left hand. Joe did not for an instant believe that he would. Honor had been satisfied. For both of them.

"Let me get you a bar towel t' wrap around that," Joe said. "An' a mug o' whiskey to help take the pain away. We'll get a doctor later if we need to."

Cy nodded. "You're a pal, Joe."

"Always will be, Cy. God knows, you've saved my bacon enough times in the past."

"Just like you done mine."

"Pull that chair out, Cy. I'll bring the whiskey." He turned away and raised his voice. "You there. Clear aside. I need to get t' the bar."

"Not in here you won't," someone called back. "Set down. We'll bring you boys your whiskey. All youse can drink."

Joe didn't figure he could reject an offer like that. He dragged a table and two chairs free of the mess he and Cy had created. He glanced toward the floor and then at Cy. "D'you want those?"

"Those what?"

"Those there." He nodded. "Your thumb an' that finger."

"Naw, I don't want 'em."

"One more thing, Cy."

"Yes?"

"You know I got t' take your scalp, don't you?"

"Jesus!" Cyrus sighed and dropped his chin. "Go ahead then. Fair is fair."

Joe took up his bowie again and leaned forward. But instead of lifting Cy's scalp, he took hold of his friend's beard and carved a few inches off the bottom, then turned and held the trophy high, to the approving laughter of the men who had watched the fight.

Blood at Bear Lake

"Damn you, Moss," Cy complained. But he was smiling when he said it, even though he was holding a bit of rag over the empty meat where a thumb and finger should have been.

"Shut up and have a drink, Cy. It'll make you feel better."

✛ 36 ✛

JOE'S HEAD HAD surely doubled in size and turned hollow. And there was some evil sonuvabitch pounding on it with drum mallets every time his heartbeat sent blood pulsing through his veins.

"Jesus, Mary, an' Joseph," he mumbled as he tried to sit up, failed, and fell back on . . . on what? Where the hell was he anyway? He could smell . . . shit. Genuinely. It smelled like somebody had crapped himself. And he could smell beer and puke and sawdust.

Which explained where he was, lying on a saloon floor. Must have passed out and spent the night there.

He tried to open his eyes, but they were pretty much glued shut. He managed to reach up, and with the fingers of his right hand—his left arm hurt too bad to move unless he really had to—pry one eye open.

That was a mistake. The light was blindingly bright. It

shot bolts of fresh pain through his skull . . . the jagged lightning of a monumental hangover.

"Oh, shit," Joe muttered aloud, squinting his eye nearly closed while he tried to calculate where he was and just how he got there.

He remembered . . . he remembered damned little actually. The fight. Celebrating after. That was in Wilson's. Was he still there? He didn't know. If the truth be told, didn't much care either. Or would not have, except that he had to take a piss. Bad. And real soon.

It would have been easier to just open up and let it flow, right there in his britches, right there on the floor.

That would have been damn-all embarrassing, though.

He forced his eyes open, blinking and squinting against the pain, and managed to roll onto his belly, then lift himself onto his hands and knees.

Cy was lying there curled up like a possum, his right hand heavily bandaged with a bar rag. One sniff told Joe that it was Cy who'd shit himself sometime during the night. He was going to for damn sure need a new pair of pants after this.

Joe noticed with some surprise that his own left arm was covered with a rag. He had almost forgotten that Cy cut him during their fight. He peeked underneath the rag and saw that some helpful soul had taken needle and thread and sewn his wound closed. Joe figured he should find out who did that and thank the man. It was a right neighborly thing for him to do.

Joe shook his head—a mistake—and blinked to clear his eyes, then with a lunge came partway onto his feet. He grabbed the seat of a chair for support and dragged himself erect. He felt ten feet tall. And wobbly.

The motion made the acids in his belly start churning.

Gary Franklin

He turned and stumbled out the back door and down the little path to the public outhouse behind Wilson's Café.

He made it there in time to avoid squirting a load into his britches the way Cy had, then turned around and puked until the only thing he would have had left to throw up was his teeth.

Joe hurried back inside—or as close to hurrying as a man in his condition could manage—and propped himself up on the end of the bar.

"Well, Moss. I see you're alive," a bartender he had never seen before said. "I would have thought that much whiskey would kill you."

"It came close. Gimme a beer, willya?"

The barman drew one and set it in front of Joe, who felt suddenly dry and empty. The beer, cool from the keg, washed some of the fur off his tongue and most of the taste of puke out of his mouth.

"Another?" the bartender asked when Joe set the empty mug down.

Joe shook his head. "One is all I need o' that."

"You aren't going to have more whiskey, are you?"

"Sonny, I may never drink whiskey again, way I feel now. It ain't good. No, what I'm wanting now is some coffee."

"No shit. Coffee?"

"This is a café, ain't it?"

"I'll make you some coffee. Pick a table. You look like you're going to fall down, the way you're swaying back and forth and hanging on to the bar. I'll bring your coffee to you. Anything else?"

"Yeah. You got any liver you could fry up for me?"

"Liver? Mister, you can't be serious."

"Serious as serious gets, sonny. I need something with strength in it. Somethin' to build up the blood. Liver's good for that. Fry me some. An' eggs. You got eggs around here?"

138

"I can find some. It will take me a few minutes, though."

"Believe me, I ain't going anywhere for a while. I'll be . . ." Joe waved a hand limply in the direction of the jumble of tables and chairs where Cyrus and a good half-dozen others were passed out on the floor. "I'll be over there."

He walked, weaving and wobbling, to the far side of the room, deliberately avoiding getting too close to Cy.

It was not that he was angry with Cy for trying to kill him. That was the right thing for his old friend to do seeing that money had changed hands already.

But, dammit, Cy stank from that load in his pants.

✢ 37 ✢

JOE GLANCED UP and smiled. "You look near about to bein' human now. Feel better, do you?"

Cy grunted.

Joe motioned Cy closer, then held up a hand to tell the man to stop while Joe tipped his head back and very loudly sniffed the air before laughing and pointing to a chair across the table from his own. "You smell better, too."

"Well, I ought to. It cost me a dollar and a half for a bath and these britches." Cy pulled the chair out and flopped into it.

"Want some o' this liver?" Joe pointed to a platter that he had not quite emptied. It held two slices of beef liver and a quantity of blood and grease to testify to those missing slabs already consumed.

Cy looked like he was going to throw up. Again. He shook his head. "I don't see how you can stand the thought o' food when my gut feels so turrible, Moss. If you was any kind of a friend, you'd be sick with me."

"Have some coffee. You'll feel better."

Cy made a face. "Coffee. Bah! You're actin' like a damned pork eater. But I'd take a whiskey if you was t' buy one."

"Sure, I'll buy your whiskey, you old fart. But listen, you ain't broke, are you? You needin' money? You know I'll share if you spent all your brass."

"Oh, hell, no. I just want you t' feel bad about my hand, that's all."

"Huh! Better your fingers than my ass, Cyrus."

"You got a point there. You really ain't mad?"

"O' course not. You took on the job. Had to do what you done afterward. I hold no hard feelin's for it."

"You're a friend, Moss. Makes me kinda glad I didn't kill you an' never mind those fingers. I'll learn t' make do."

The bartender came to the table, and Joe asked for more coffee and a bottle of whiskey. The barman went away shaking his head at these uncivilized old mountain men. He did not often see their kind in the city.

"Thinkin' about money reminds me," Cy said. "The fella that hired me t' lay for whoever it was that blew up the Peabody mine."

"What about him?"

"He wasn't satisfied with havin' me wait here. He said he was going on over to Colorado an' then up into Wyoming to hire some other fellas, not just me. Whichever one of us kil't you was t' get a bonus. Another thousand dollars."

"Damn," Joe mumbled. "Any way you could know who these others are or where they'll be?"

Cy shook his head. "If I knew, I'd for damn sure tell you, but I don't. I don't think he knew himself. He was just gonna look around when he got to these different spots where he thought you might show up. That's what he done here when he hired me."

"I've had better news, but I'll handle things as I come to them. No need to borrow trouble. Here you go, Cy. Here's that whiskey you wanted." Joe dug into his pouch to pay for his meal and for Cy's bottle.

"How are ya feelin' now, pard?" Joe asked solicitously. They were alone behind the livery stable where Joe's big Shire was boarded. He had been buying Cy's whiskey for more than an hour. Joe himself had had nothing but coffee.

"I'm good. Yeah. I am."

The man didn't *look* good. He looked about half-drunk again. But alert and able to talk. Just loosened up a little. Perfect.

"You got to tell me more about this guy offering t' pay for my killing, Cy."

"Course I'll tell my ol' pard. Whadaya wanna know?"

"You was to wait for me and kill me, right?"

"Tha's right." Cy nodded and belched. For a moment, Joe thought he had misjudged and Cyrus was going to puke and pass out, but the old mountain man only blinked and swayed back and forth a little.

"Was there anything else?"

"Jeez, Joe, ain't killin' enough for ye?"

"I mean was there any*body* else, Cy? Were you fellows supposed to look for anybody else, too?"

"Oh, that. Well, yeah, but that don't have nothing t' do with you, does it?"

"Maybe. Tell me about it."

"Well the thing is . . . I'm kinda emba . . . embar . . ."

"Embarrassed, yeah. Go on."

"There was somethin' about watching for some woman, too. Redheaded woman. An' a kid. But that was separate, see, an' not so much money promised for th . . . th . . . for them. Joe, lemme sit down over here for a minute, can I?"

"Sure, Cy. Let me help you." Joe put an arm over Cy's shoulders and guided him to some discarded kegs, helped him to a secure seat on one of them.

"Thanks." Cy belched again. When he looked up, he said with a note of querulous surprise, "Joe, where you goin', eh? We got more drinkin' t' do."

But Joe Moss either failed to hear his old friend, or simply ignored him. Joe was headed for the stall where his horse was.

He seemed to be in a hurry.

✢ 38 ✢

A N OLD MAN with thinning gray hair and a pair of prissy spectacles perched on the bridge of his nose sat in a rocking chair in front of a dusty, ramshackle building. A sign pegged into the adobe over his head read: TRADING POST.

One lone horse, its ribs showing and its mane tangled, stood hipshot and head down in a corral adjacent to the single-story building. An American flag hung limp atop a tall post in front of the corral.

Joe stopped a few feet away from the scrawny old man. He grunted and said, "Gabe, you look like a damned old snapping turtle sunning hisself on a mossy rock. I woulda thought you'd've died years back."

"Hell, Moss, what I heard was that you'd went under afore me. Step down off that"—he cocked his head to one side and squinted—"whatever that big sumbich is . . . get down off it an' come inside. We'll have us a drink an' talk about how it was when the beaver was plenty an' the squaws cheap." He dug a finger inside his beard and scratched, then shook his head. "First time I ever seen a mountain grow legs an' move."

"Hell, Gabe, what this is is two horses. Brothers actually. Looked just alike. It's just that I was trailing the one behind the other on a real short tether. The one in front seen something on the ground an' spooked. Tried to back away. Same time, the one in back heard somethin' and jumped forward. Jumped right up the other'n's ass. Well the two of them was like enough that he disappeared inside an' just stayed there. But all filled out, like. So what you see here is really the two o' them animals stuffed t'gether inta one. I swear it t' be true."

"An' I believe you. Damn me if'n I don't." The smaller man, a head shorter than Joe but wiry and agile, grabbed Joe in a bear hug. Had Joe Moss been a weaker man, he might have cracked some ribs.

The legendary mountain man Jim Bridger, Old Gabe to his friends, stepped back and squinted through his schoolmarm spectacles, looking Joe over from toe to head and back again. "You look good, boy. Y' look fit. D'you be looking for a job? I heard o' one that pays real good."

"I got no time for work right now, Gabe. My wife and me got separated. I got t' find her. Even more, I got to find the sonuvabitch that's offering a bounty on her head. Mine, too, but that don't matter. I can take care o' myself. It's Fiona that I'm worried about."

"Shit!" Jim Bridger snarled.

"Why'd you say that, Gabe? What's the matter?"

"You're married, Joe? Got you a wife name of Fiona?"

"That's right."

"Redheaded girl, is she?"

"Yeah, but how did you know that?"

"Because the young fella that's offering the bounty come through here. Shit, that's the job of work I was thinkin' to offer you."

"Gabe, you aren't . . ."

"Oh, hell, no, I ain't shilling for him and I don't got no stake in it m'self. He asked me did I know of anybody could do the job. I told him I prob'ly know half a hundred fellows what were capable of it, but right off hand I didn't know of any that was looking for work nor where any of them was. You're the first man t' come along that I thought could handle that kind of work if he was of a mind to." Bridger shook his head. "You wouldn't believe the run of Bible-thumpers and just plain cowards that been coming through here, runnin' toward Californy, ever since that war got started back East. They come an' they gawk an' they buy stuff from me just so they can say they met Old Jim Bridger an' sat on his front porch. Well, I can tell you one thing. Ain't one of them gets invited to set in my kitchen an' have a drink or a plate o' beans with me." He cackled and added, "Joe Moss, c'mon into my place. We'll go in back and set in the kitchen while my woman fixes us something to eat. Maybe some ribs t' go with those beans."

"Yeah. Yeah, I'd be proud t' do that, Gabe. But if you don't mind, I'd like you t' tell me whatever else you can about this fella that's spreading the word about a bounty on me an' my wife."

"Figure to go kill the son of a bitch, do ye, son?"

"You know that I do, Gabe."

"Moss, had I knowed the way the stick floats, I'd've killed him for ye. An' if he comes back this way, I damn sure will."

Blood at Bear Lake

"You're a friend, Gabe. Thanks. Just let me tend to my horse an' mule, then we'll tell some lies about how it was in the Shining Times."

"Shit, you can lie if you like, Moss, but everything I say is the truth, nothing but the purantee truth." Jim Bridger winked and said, "Count on it."

✣ 39 ✣

OLD HABITS DIE hard. That was the common expression. That was the truth.

Moss kicked apart the tiny fire he had built to quickly cook his supper, then mounted the Shire and moved on another half mile before he stopped to make his camp for the night. Joe did not know of any specific danger hereabouts, but he had lived so much of his life in the presence of danger that he remained constantly on guard out of sheer habit.

He removed his panniers from the mule's packsaddle and set them down, one on either side of where he would bed, then pulled the pack frame from the animal and fitted hobbles to its feet before turning it loose to graze. Then he removed his saddle from the big black and gave it a rubdown before hobbling it and letting it graze.

He spread his blankets between the panniers—in the event of attack in the night they would provide a barricade of sorts—and placed the saddle for use as his pillow. He needed no other comforts.

The spot he chose to spend the night was well away from wood or water. There was nothing that should attract the attention of travelers in the vicinity, and that was how he liked it.

Joe did permit himself a final pipe during the waning moments of a long day. He sat cross-legged at the foot of his blanket, savoring the taste of the smoke in his mouth. While he sat there, he thought back to what Jim Bridger told him.

"This man that's put the bounty on you an' your missus, Joe. He's a hard case. The real thing. He has the look of a man that's lifted hair hisself. He don't just hire it done by others. You know the look I mean."

"I do," Joe had answered his old friend. "Those of us that survived the old days, we all got that look ourselves."

"Now I don't say this fella went through the exact same things that we done. He didn't. You and me would know him if he did. But he ain't a stranger when it comes to hard living and dirty fighting. I'd say this man knows how to handle a knife or a gun, either one.

"His name is Ransom Holt. Calls himself the chief of security for some fella name of Peabody, and he likes to show a badge. Just a flash of it, though, quick before a body has a chance to wonder if it's an official badge or not. Fact is, it ain't. Which he will admit once he knows he ain't gonna too easy pull the wool over your eyes.

"This Holt is a big man, Moss. Half a head taller than you. And he's built like a damn oak tree. Solid. Long arms. You don't want him to get his hands on you, or you're likely done. You don't want to fight him with a knife either, not with arms like that. Big as he is, he moves pretty good. Not clumsy at all. If you run into him, Moss, stay back and use your rifle. And don't stop shooting till you've tore him to pieces. I have it in mind that this Holt will be hard to kill."

"I'm not so easy t' kill my own self, Gabe."

"I know that, Joe, but I don't have so many friends that I want to see any more of them go under. You watch out for yourself when you come up against Holt."

"If I ever do."

"Don't lie to me, Moss. You know an' I know, too. You are going to keep after Holt for as long as he's a threat to you and your wife. You won't quit until one of you is laying dead on the ground."

Joe had only grunted and nodded. Bridger was right. Ransom Holt—and the Peabodys who backed him—threatened Fiona's life and perhaps the life of Joe's daughter, Jessica, as well. Joe could not permit that.

He could put up with any threat on his own life. He could scarcely remember a time when he had not had to be wary of dangers that could easily and without warning put him under.

But Fiona? And Jessica? They were precious beyond measure and there was no length he would not go to in order to protect them.

He needed to find Fiona.

No, he amended to himself as he puffed quietly on his pipe, he *wanted* to find Fiona.

He *needed* to kill Ransom Holt. That was the only sure way he could think of to remove future threats to his beloved wife and daughter.

According to Bridger, the head of security for the Peabody mines had been heading east with the intention of visiting some of the places where a man on the run might logically show up. A former mountain man.

That would certainly include Fort Laramie on the emigrant wagon route. Probably the Bayou Salado and Fountain Creek down in Colorado. Taos and Santa Fe in Mexico. No, dammit, they were in the United States now. Sometimes he tended to forget that.

When he thought about it, there was an awful lot of prime country he and the other boys used to roam back in the days when fur was king and they were the lords of the mountains.

Remembering those days, Joe permitted himself a small smile.

Then he sobered. Fiona. He had to think of Fiona and Jessica. He had to protect them from this Ransom Holt.

Grim and determined, Joe knocked the dottle from his pipe and dropped it back into his possibles pouch, then took one long, cautious look around, searching for the sight or the scent of an enemy, before lying down for the night.

✦ 40 ✦

F ORT LARAMIE HAD not changed much since the last
time Joe was there. It was perhaps busier thanks to increased traffic on the old Oregon Trail, but it was no
grander. The few buildings were weathered, the logs warp-
ing and adobe brick melting.

But there were pens of livestock—oxen, mules, and heavy
horses taken in on trade and allowed to recuperate here
while their former owners traveled on to California and
Oregon and Deseret—and sheds where goods were either
stored or manufactured. There were a leatherworks and harness maker, a blacksmith, a low shed where bunks could be
hired with or without a plump Shoshone girl to warm a
man's blankets . . . and whatever.

There was the usual assortment of white and red inhab-
itants, almost enough to make a small town out of what was
initially only a trading point for mountain men and the occasional emigrant. Now it seemed that the emigrant trains

had become the majority. And a busy traffic they were providing. The place swarmed with wagons and draft stock and the curses of bullwhackers.

Joe stopped at one of the many corrals only long enough to put his horse and mule in and strip their gear. Then, his heart in his throat at the prospect of finding Fiona again, he hurried to the trading post where he had so many memories from the past.

The place was very much as he remembered it. Low, dim, smelling of whiskey and cured fur and tobacco. Goods were piled on shelves and stacked on the floor, and there must have been three dozen people crowded inside looking to buy or to trade for whatever they needed to go onward.

Joe wove his way through the crowd, sliding this way and that and becoming impatient at the pork-eating sons of bitches who were in his way now that he might at last find Fiona.

"Move, dammit!"

A pasty-faced man with stringy hair bristled at being so ordered. He spun around ready to fight, but one look at Joe Moss's face convinced him that would not be a good idea. The fellow wilted and scurried out of Joe's path.

Joe stepped up to the counter and eyed the middle-aged clerk who stood behind it.

"Where's Sol?" he demanded.

"Who?" the clerk said.

"Sol, dammit. Sol Pennington. He's your boss here, ain't he? So where is the old sonuvabitch?" Sol Pennington was an old and true friend, a former mountain man himself who had helped Joe recover from the bender he had gone on when he first lost Fiona some years back. Joe was looking forward to seeing Sol again.

"Oh, yes. Of course." The clerk shook his head. "Pennington was gone before I got here."

"Gone? Where the hell's he gone?"

"Gone like in dead, mister. Pennington got himself killed."

The news hit Joe harder than he would have believed. He grounded the butt of his Henry rifle on the trading post floor and reached out to touch the counter. He needed to take hold of something solid in a suddenly dizzying world.

Sol had come through more Indian fights than most men had ever heard tales about. He had saved Joe's life many times over. And Joe had saved his in return. Now . . . dead?

"How?" Joe asked. "How'd old Sol go under?"

The clerk shrugged, not particularly interested in the topic. "He back-talked some customer, I think. The customer killed him."

"Shot him?" Joe asked.

"Knife, I think."

Joe frowned. Sol was a canny old wolf. He would not have been easy to take any way at all, but . . . a knife? Unless it was in the back, Joe would not have thought that possible.

"What about Sol? Did he get his licks in? Did he at least take the pilgrim with him?"

"Mister, I wouldn't know about that shit, and I don't have time to stand here jawing with you to no purpose. If you want to buy something, fine. Otherwise, please stand aside so's I can take care of these other folks."

Joe wanted to ask about Fiona, too. But not of this snotty son of a bitch. Surely there would be others hanging on from the old days. He would question any of those that he came to. In the meantime, he would drift through the compound and see if he could spot Fiona or her pretty little sorrel.

He turned away from the counter, his eyes moving back

and forth over the crowd, searching for a familiar face among all these strangers.

But old Sol. Dead. Joe could scarcely believe it.

Henri Valderama was noisily engaged in trying to barter a pair of poor-quality wolf skins to a family of Easterners whose three boys were wide-eyed at the yarn Valderama was spinning in an effort to get a good price for the skins. Likely the trading post had already refused them, so now he was trying to unload them on the pilgrims.

Joe walked close by, looking and listening as he did so. He was tempted to stop and ask Henri about Fiona, but stifled the impulse. Henri likely had not spoken a true thing since he told his mama he was leaving home thirty or forty years ago. Anything Valderama might say would almost certainly be a lie anyway, so why bother?

He wandered back past the pigpens—oh, they brought back memories: laying up drunk and crawling into the hog house on hands and knees to share the warmth given off by the hogs' bodies—and saw a fat, homely squaw squatting in the dirt to take a piss.

She looked up, saw him, and began to grin. Quickly, she finished, gave a little wiggle of her hips to shake herself off, then stood and came trotting toward him.

Probably looking for a handout was his first thought. Then she called out, "Hel-lo, Man Killer." It was a name he had been given long ago and was known by among the Indian tribes. Damned few white men would know it, though, especially now when he had been away from the mountains for so long.

There was something about the woman's voice . . . something familiar. And her face . . . Joe cocked his head and half-closed one eye as he took a closer look.

Joe broke into a grin. "Lulu!" he yelped, and gathered her into a bear hug.

Nine or ten years back, Lulu was a slim and pretty Mandan girl who had been captured by the Lakota and kept as a slave. Joe bought her out of captivity for use as a "winter wife" one year. She was a hard worker and a fine fuck. Come spring, he had married her off to a young Cheyenne who did not own enough horses to buy a wife among his own people. Yeah, he remembered Lulu.

"How've you been, Lulu? Where is your husband?" Joe could not remember the young brave's name, but he did not want to say so.

"He is dead. Rubbed out. Baby dead, too." She shrugged. "Now I am here. Work hard." She brightened. "You want wife, Man Killer? You know I am good wife."

"I know you're a fine wife, Lulu, but I already got a wife. White woman. She wouldn't understand me takin' another wife, too."

"Oh." Lulu did not look overly disappointed by the news.

"Maybe you've seen my wife, Lulu. Her and me got separated so now I'm lookin' to find her. Maybe here. You been here at the fort long?"

"I live here, Man Killer. Here three, maybe four winter."

"Then you might've seen her. White woman about this tall." He held his hand to indicate Fiona's height. "Long red hair. Pale complexion with freckles."

"Freck . . . what are them?"

"Little dots on the face. Like tiny flecks of paint but they don't wash off."

"Oh, yes. I know."

"You know her? You've seen her?" Joe's excitement rose at the prospect of being reunited with his darling, then was quickly dashed when Lulu said, "I know what you mean by freck, not know white woman with red hair."

"Damn! You haven't seen anyone like that?"

Lulu shook her head.

"All right, thanks. Say, you've been here awhile, so that means you was here when Sol was killed. D'you know what happened to him?"

"Huh! Sol, he was good to me. Gave me work when did not need work. You know what I mean?"

"I do, Lulu. Sol was a good man. A good friend."

"This new man"—she made a sour face and spat—"he is not a good man, Man Killer. Not good. No work for me, none."

"That's a shame, Lulu. I'm sorry 'bout that. But you was gonna tell me about Sol."

She shrugged. "A man comes. Big man. He is hunting someone. Show Sol a metal star, very shiny and pretty. I see it myself. I am standing in the store. Going to ask Sol for work. I do not hear what they spoke of, but Sol gets angry. Tells the big man to go. They argue. Yell. Back and forth. Back and forth. The big man has a knife. He cuts Sol. So." Lulu ran her index finger across her more-than-ample belly and made a swishing sound.

"Sol's guts fall out. The big man takes a bottle from behind counter, then goes to a table and speaks with other white men. Sol tries to catch his guts and push them back inside, but pretty soon he falls down. They say he dies next day sometime, but I was not there when he dies, Man Killer, so I cannot say about that, no."

"Dammit, Lulu, Sol was a good friend o' mine. I want you to tell me more about what this big man looks like an' who it was he talked to after he cut Sol."

"I will tell, Man Killer, but do you want fuck? You know I am good."

"I know you are, sweetheart, and I'm gonna give you some money t' help you out, but right now what I most need from you is a real good description of this big man that killed Sol."

"Over here, Man Killer. Come over here. We will sit and we will talk, eh?"

✦ 41 ✦

Ransom Holt. It was the Peabody head of security who killed Sol. The same son of a bitch who was putting a price on Joe's head. And on Fiona's.

Joe could forgive the man for trying to kill him. Could even accept his having killed Sol, for Sol was a man grown and well capable of defending himself. But Fiona! There was no power on earth that could make Joe forgive Holt—or anyone else—for seeking to harm his beloved Fiona.

Or anyone else, he reminded himself.

Ransom Holt was but a cur dog doing his master's bidding, and that master would be a Peabody.

By Joe's reckoning, there should be only one of the Peabody brothers left alive after the carnage he had brought upon them back in Nevada. That was one Peabody too many. They were the cause of Fiona's troubles, falsely accusing her of murdering one of their own and siccing the law on her when they knew she was innocent. Now they continued to threaten the lives of Fiona and of little Jessica.

Joe intended to do something about that.

But first things first.

He had to find Fiona. It worried him to be apart from her and unable to protect her from Holt and his hired thugs. Jessica was safe enough, at least for the time being, in the convent back in Nevada where Fiona had left her. The responsibility for protecting both of them lay on Joe's shoulders, however.

He needed first to find Fiona. Then to stop Holt from engaging assassins who wanted to lift Joe's hair and to kill or capture Fiona and Jessica, too. Joe had to find Ransom Holt. He had to kill the man. That was the only sure way to stop him. That was exactly what Joe intended to do.

But, dammit, he was in the middle of a dilemma. On the one hand, he needed to be here at Fort Laramie where he believed Fiona was headed. On the other, he needed to find this Holt son of a bitch, and, according to Lulu, Holt had already moved on, headed south into what they were nowadays calling Colorado. Denver, Fountain Creek, the Bayou Salado maybe.

Holt was probably planting seeds of treachery. Leaving them behind him wherever he had been, men who were told what to look for and what reward they could expect if they succeeded in killing Joe or Fiona.

Cy Brainard back in Salt Lake City had been the first of Holt's would-be killers that Joe encountered. It was not likely that Cy would be the last.

Joe sat cross-legged on the ground, leaning back against a fence post on the corral where his horse and mule were confined. He loaded his pipe with tobacco and used a burning glass to light it, then sat slowly puffing the tasty smoke.

To all outward appearances, he seemed a man who was half asleep and paying no mind to what was around him.

He was anything but inattentive, however, his senses alert to danger and his thoughts churning.

If he left immediately to catch up with and kill Ransom Holt, he would be leaving Fiona on her own that much longer. But if he waited to find Fiona, Joe would only be giving Holt that much longer to sow his seeds of murder.

Joe grunted and dropped the half-smoked pipe back into his possibles pouch. He stood and brushed off the seat of his britches.

Regardless of what he decided between those choices, he realized, there was something more immediate that needed his attention.

There was someone—somewhere—here amid the crowds and confusion of Fort Laramie—who intended to kill him.

He was sure of that. Otherwise, Ransom Holt would not have left to head south. Fort Laramie was one of the major stops on the Oregon Trail, and anyone crossing the plains in either direction was sure to come through. It only stood to reason that Holt would not have left the post without hiring at least one killer to wait here and to watch.

Joe checked his revolver to make sure the caps were all properly in place, then loosened the bowie in its sheath and touched the head of his tomahawk to make sure everything was correctly placed. If he needed any of his weapons, they had to come to hand without any fumbling or uncertainty because there might very well be no warning before Holt's snakes struck.

Then he set off, seemingly relaxed and aimless, to smoke out whoever it was at the post who wanted his head.

✤ 42 ✤

A T THE END of a long day of questioning strangers and a handful of acquaintances from his old days in the mountains, Joe knew nothing more than he had already learned from Lulu.

He was sure Ransom Holt would not have left Fort Laramie without hiring an assassin, but he had no idea who that person might be.

He was equally sure—no, upon reflection not equally, but reasonably sure—that Fiona was likely to come here in an effort to find him.

After all, Fiona would be looking for him just as surely as he was anxious to reunite with her. The two of them were one person, man and wife, and they needed to be together so they could reclaim Jessica from the convent and make a life together as a family.

Fort Laramie was one of the few places Fiona would associate with Joe. He tried to think back to the conversations they had had in the brief period when they were together after that first awful separation.

They had talked. Of course they had talked. But more about her ordeal than about his life before they married.

Had he mentioned Santa Fe and his days as a bull-whacker and wagon master? He could not recall.

Certainly there were things he had done—and women he had bedded—that he would not want to discuss with Fiona. Oh, if she ever directly asked, he would be honest about those days. He would tell her rather than lie, for a good marriage cannot be built on a bed of lies. But unless she directly questioned him about those times, well, there was no point in bringing them up when he did not have to.

Thinking back to the women he had known then, Joe now felt his manhood lengthen and swell inside his britches. It was time to change the direction of his thinking before he went and did something he might regret afterward. Not all the Indian girls who were here were as fat and homely as Lulu, and Joe could have had almost any of them for a kind word and a few twists of tobacco. It was difficult to keep from remembering that.

In past times, he would have had a bottle in one hand and a red-hued breast in the other by the time the sun went down.

Which it was soon going to do. Joe tilted his head and squinted, staring off toward the west where the sun was disappearing beneath the horizon. Lost in thought, he stood like that for a moment. Then visibly shook himself as he came back to the here and now of his situation.

He slipped inside the corral where his Shire and the mule were lodged, and gave them each a brief rubdown. He bought some grain from a Kansas mule packer and gave it to his animals to go along with the wild grass hay that was already available in a rick. By that time it was dark, and there was a chill in the air.

Another day had passed with no sign of Fiona. Dammit!

Joe strode to the trading post and pushed his way through the knot of emigrants, Kentuckians these were, who were gathered outside.

"Whiskey," he roared as he approached the counter. "Two bottles o' whiskey. None o' that fancy shit now. Injun whiskey is good enough for Old Joe Moss." He banged the flat of his hand on the counter. "I been drinking Injun whiskey since before you was born, sonny. No reason for me t' change now." He banged the counter again and laid a tiny gold quarter eagle down to pay for it. "Two bottles, I said. One for me and one for them boys outside. They look like they could use a drink, too."

"Two bottles it is." The clerk brought them and picked up Joe's money. Indian whiskey should have been no more than a dollar a bottle, but he did not offer any change. The man peered closely into Joe's face for a moment, then asked, "You're Moss, ain't you?"

"That's right. That mean something t' you, mister?"

"No. I asked after you were in here looking for Pennington, that's all. They said you used to be a real he-coon."

"That's right. Still am, too." Joe pulled the cork from one of the brown bottles and took a slug of the cheap trade whiskey. He coughed and half-choked, spitting at least half of it back out again. "By God," he roared, "you people here ain't learned to make any better Injun whiskey than you ever did. An' don't be telling me what's in it. If you did tell me the truth, I wouldn't wanta know it." He took a more moderate drink. "Snake shit an' turtle turds is what it tastes like." He grinned. "But it's whiskey. Damn me if it ain't."

Joe turned around and weaved his way unsteadily outside. He did not remember to stop and give the extra bottle to the gents gathered just outside the door, but carried it on with him toward the corral where his horse and mule were confined.

Moss was accustomed to being alone anyway. And two bottles ought to be enough company for anyone.

✦ 43 ✦

"SHH! WATCH WHERE ya step."

"Shush yer own damn self, Carl. You an' them big feet o' yorn."

"Where the hell is this fella, Asa?"

"The man said someplace out this-a here way. After two bottles, he should ought fer t' be layin' up drunk by now."

"You hope. You ain't never killed nobody afore now."

"Well, you ain't neither. Besides, I ain't scared to. Not for that kinda money, I ain't."

"Hush now, dammit, lest he hears you."

"You're the one makin' all the noise."

"Whoa. Is that him?"

"I don't see nothin'."

"Over by that fence line yonder."

"Looks like a shadow to me."

"He's got to be right close aroun' here someplace, Asa."

"So watch yer step now. Slow an' easy does it. Slow an'

easy. Don't make no noise. It'll be easy. One whack o' the ax an' all that money's our'n, just like the man said. Easy money, Carl. Easy money."

"I sure as shit hope it's easy."

"Aw, it ain't gonna be no worse 'n killin' a shoat. Easier likely. This fella ain't gonna be runnin' around no pen an' squealin'. He'll just be laying there passed out from that likker."

"Lordy, I could use a drink my own self."

"Soon as we collect our money, we'll both of us have a drink. Likely more'n one."

"Shh. Shh. I think I see him. Right over there in that shadow. Y'see? D' you see?"

"Right. Shush now. You got that ax ready? All right. Now quiet, boy. Real, real quiet. No, stop. Wait just a minute whilst I get my breathin' slowed down. What we can do, we'll slip in just a little bit closer, then rush the son of a bitch. Run in quick and one whack and it's done. Right?"

"I'm nervous."

"Shit, there ain't nothing t' be scared of. The man is passed out drunk. You can see for yourself."

"Yeah. I see."

"All right now. Ready with the ax. Get set . . . *go!*"

✛ 44 ✛

JOE SAT COMFORTABLY enough with his back against a feed bunk inside the next corral over from where he had laid out his gear. He was a little cool—felt like he was damned well freezing actually—because his blankets, hat, and rifle were laid out on the ground where they could be seen if anyone took the bait he was dangling there for them. This chill was nothing, though, compared with wading thigh-deep in a cold mountain stream to check a set of beaver traps. Nor did it rise to the level of danger he had faced one night on the Musselshell when half a dozen pissed-off Crow warriors were searching for him. Both parties, then and now, were after his scalp.

That was a thing to keep in mind, Joe told himself.

Take an enemy lightly and you give him an edge. Enemies could indeed be dismissed as unimportant, Joe figured . . . after they were dead.

He sat motionless in the shadows, virtually under the bellies of a dozen or so mules that were part of some freighter's string. He would not have trusted himself like that to oxen nor even to horses, but mules are cautious about where they place their feet. He was in no danger from the mules. In fact, the long-eared beasts were acting as his sentinels. Their hearing was as acute as any dog's, and they were not so vocal in their warnings when someone passed near.

A dozen times or more, the mules warned Joe that someone was coming. Almost as one, their ears swiveled and pointed, telling Joe not only that someone was close, but pinpointing exactly where.

People came and went, passing on in whatever business they had in the night. Joe sat and waited. And watched.

"Shit, there ain't nothing t' be scared of. The man is passed out drunk. You can see for yourself."

"Yeah. I see."

Joe heard the whispers. He did not recognize the voices. He did recognize the threat, however.

There were two of them. One was carrying an ax, a single-bit blade of the kind someone might use to chop firewood. The other seemed to have a club, or perhaps simply a section of tree limb.

Joe was mildly surprised that this particular pair had been hired as assassins. They did not appear to be well suited to the task. They lacked the degree of stealth that Indian fighters develop—or at least those who survive long enough to learn—nor did they exhibit any firearms. Joe would have thought that in a frontier post like Fort Laramie, Ransom Holt could have found someone more likely to succeed than these two.

Not that Joe was complaining. Hell, he hoped all of Holt's choices were this inept.

The two of them crept up on Joe's blankets with no more noise and commotion than a team of dray horses might have made. When they were in position to make their final rush, they stopped. He got the idea that they needed a moment to screw up their courage—much of which probably came from a whiskey bottle to begin with—and prepare themselves to commit murder.

Murder is not an easy thing, Joe figured.

Killing is something else again. There are many reasons that can make it necessary to kill another human. Joe had done that many times and never regretted it afterward. If it was genuinely necessary, there was no cause for regret; if it was not necessary, he did not do it. Plain and simple.

What these two men were preparing themselves to do was murder.

They intended to attack and to kill a sleeping man who was no threat to them whatsoever—or would not have been had they not chosen to come after him in the night—and they intended to do that not for cause, but for money.

Joe did not know what Ransom Holt was offering in exchange for his scalp.

But it was not enough.

As the assassins crept ever closer to Joe's empty blankets, he stirred a little, giving the mules around him time to recognize the fact that their visitor was moving.

The mules parted, stepping carefully aside as Joe uncoiled from his position beside the feed bunk.

He slipped silently through the bars of the corral, and came out behind the two who wanted to murder him.

The taller of the two paused and took a deep breath as if to steel his nerve.

"All right now. Ready with the ax. Get set . . . *go!*"

✦ 45 ✦

IT WAS JOE MOSS who "went." Joe stepped in close behind the one in the rear, the taller of the two. He was the
one who was wielding the club, which up close Joe could
now see was a singletree that was part of someone's hitch.

The shorter man hefted his ax and stepped confidently
toward the still form on the ground, thinking it was Joe lying
there passed out and defenseless.

Joe, in fact, was not quite so defenseless as these boys
seemed to think he was.

While the fellow with the ax was busy planting his heavy
blade square into the top of Joe's hat, a killing blow for certain had it been Joe lying there and not a makeshift dummy,
Joe was taking a swing with his own very much smaller ax.

Joe's tomahawk reflected sharp sparkles of starlight as
he deftly chopped the back of the tall man's neck, severing
the spine and killing the son of a bitch instantly.

The man fell, the singletree he had been carrying falling with a dull clatter.

Even before his dead partner hit the ground, the shorter fellow with the ax felt by the impact that his blade had not found flesh nor bone, but only a nearly empty flour sack that Joe had propped his hat on.

He took his ax up, but did not strike again. That was when he turned around and saw his partner lying dead on the ground and someone else standing over the body. "Hey, dammit!"

"Hey yourself, you piece o' shit," Joe barked. "You've gone an' ruint a perfectly good hat, damn you."

"Who . . . ?" The fellow's eyes went wide with shocked realization at what was happening. "Look . . . mister, I . . . I . . . oh, shit!" He let the ax hang at his side.

The fellow seemed to steel himself. He paused for only a moment, then exploded into motion, bringing the ax up again and lashing out with a quick, sweeping stroke that would have spilled Joe's guts onto the ground if it had connected.

Instead, the sharp blade swept harmlessly through nothing but air where Joe's belly had been a moment earlier.

The emigrant grunted with the effort of his blow, his breath whooshing loud from his lungs in the silence of the night. Joe could smell the garlic he had had in his last meal.

Last meal indeed!

Joe stepped in behind the emigrant's missed ax stroke, stepped in close, and quickly hacked once with his already bloody tomahawk. Joe's blade cut through flesh and sinew and bone, and the heavy ax fell onto the ground, dropping from suddenly nerveless fingers as the fellow's arm was chopped very nearly in two just above the wrist. What was left dangled and flopped, useless and spouting blood that was black and shiny in the dim starlight.

"Oh, God!" The man screamed and grabbed his wrist with his other hand, trying to stanch the flow.

Joe moved sideways a step and then another, trying to see what other armaments the man might have on him.

Not that it would have mattered anyway. The fellow was out of this fight, and probably everything else as well. His horrified concentration was focused totally on his grievously wounded right hand. Joe doubted he would have noticed had a herd of naked doxies paraded themselves before him pleading for his attention.

"You're gonna bleed t' death," Joe said, shoving his tomahawk casually into his sash. He bent and picked up his hat, scowled at the clean slice this man's ax had put into the felt, and punched it back into shape before putting it on again. He hated going bareheaded in the night air. Bad for the lungs, or so he believed, and left a man susceptible to all manner of ills and influenzas.

He stepped closer to the injured man and repeated, slower and a little louder this time, "You are gonna bleed to death, mister." This time the man seemed to hear.

"I . . . I . . . oh, God!"

"You already said that. I don't know as it's doing you any good."

"But I . . . I . . ."

"Point that blood spray somewheres else, will ya? I don't want t' get it all over me."

"Jesus, mister, I'm dying here and you're taking it awful light."

"Well, I reckon so. Mister, I'm the one you just now tried t' kill. You want sympathy, this ain't the place to get it."

"Help me, mister. You got to help me."

"All I *got* t' do is stand here an' watch you die. That an' tell folks that I'm proud to be the one that's killed you. Or I *could* take my belt . . . no, wait a minute, no sense in that . . .

173

I could take *his* belt"—he pointed to the dead man lying at his feet—"I could take his belt an' tie off your arm so's you don't bleed out. Then you and me could have a little talk about why it was you decided you wanted t' come along an' kill me while I was laying there passed out drunk."

"You could do that?"

"Ayuh. Could. But I ain't saying that I would. Why the hell should I?" Joe snorted. "Unless you was to tell me some things."

"Anything," the man frantically said.

It was plain to see that the grip of the man's good hand was weakening with the blood loss and that soon he would have no effect at all on the continuing dark flow from his slippery, blood-slick arm.

"Here," Joe said. "This might help." He rather delicately took the injured hand by one finger and held it so he could critically examine the strip of flesh and tendons that kept the hand so tenuously attached to the fellow's forearm. After a moment, Joe said, "Uh-huh," and used his razor-sharp bowie to deftly slice through the last strips of flesh. The severed hand dropped to the ground and the emigrant screamed again.

"Should be easier t' tie off now," Joe said. He smiled. "If I want t' bother stopping you from bleedin' to death. Can you think of any reason why I should?"

"I . . . I . . . anything, mister. Anything. But you got to help me. You got to."

"First you tell me why you come at me like you done. Then we'll see do I want t' bother stopping you from dyin'. Set down. You're starting t' look a little pale. Set down by that post there . . . no, not on my blankets, dammit, you'll get 'em all bloody . . . set an' tell me what I'm wantin' t' know."

J OE HUMMED A Lakota chant while he gathered up his
  things and moved them away from the blood and the
two bodies. Stupid sons of bitches! They had thought to
strike it rich without even going to California. Instead, they
reached the end of their road right here at Fort Laramie.

According to the one with the ax, each left a wife and
family back in wherever the fuck they came from. Those
wives likely would never know what happened to their hus-
bands. Just as well that they didn't, Joe thought with a
grunt as he placed his blankets and saddle down again.

He patted his war bag, which now held two fresh scalps
to add to his collection. He would have to remember to
dry these. Fiona had not liked the smell of his old scalps
and threw them away. Maybe if he properly dressed this
new and still growing collection, she would not mind having them around. In Joe's opinion, a man just naturally felt

better having those reminders of past success close to hand for him to sing about.

By the time Joe was done, it was closer to dawn than to dusk. He could feel the chill of the morning air, and he shivered just a little as he strode through the darkness toward the old trading post that had been Sol Pennington's. And Burl Danforth's before Sol, and . . . it took him a moment to call back to mind the name of the long-dead trader who had had the post before Danforth. Jones. Reggie Jones that had been. All of them dead and gone now.

The place was shut down for the night, the last of the drunks thrown out and the heavy door barred, although there was a rim of yellow lamplight around the edges of the door. Likely, the proprietor was busy cleaning up. Or counting his profits.

Joe took his bowie out and used the heavy butt end to rap on the door. Loud and hard.

There was no immediate response, so he did it again, and kept up the pounding until he heard a voice from the other side call out, "I'm closed, dammit. Come back in the morning."

"I have an express packet for someone name of James Tuttle," Joe called through the door.

"An express?"

"That's right. Some fella in Julesburg paid me t' carry it here. I'm supposed to give it into the hand of this James Tuttle person an' no other. That's what I was told."

"But what is it?"

"How the hell would I know? The package is tied tight with string. It ain't heavy enough t' be gold, though." He faked a laugh. "I don't know as it woulda got here if I thought it was gold."

"Just a minute, then." There was the thump and scrape of a heavy bar being retracted, then the door swung partially open. "Let me have . . . *you*!" The trader's eyes went wide when he saw who his nocturnal visitor was.

Joe shouldered his way inside, pulling the door closed behind him. He yanked the bar into place, locking himself inside with James Tuttle, who turned out to be the same impatient fellow Joe had spoken with earlier in the day, the one who took Sol's place when Sol was murdered by Ransom Holt.

"What do you want here? Come back during business hours and we . . ."

Joe shut him up with a slap across the face.

"Wh—you can't do that!"

Joe slapped him again. Harder. Blood began to trickle out of the corner of Tuttle's mouth.

"Why are you . . . why are you doing this?" Tuttle demanded. His voice was firm. But he did not meet Joe's eyes when he spoke. He knew damned good and well why Joe was there.

Joe slapped him a third time, the force of it turning Tuttle half around. His hand crept into the pocket of his apron and emerged holding a tiny pepperbox revolver.

Joe took it away from him.

Tuttle turned pale with terror now that he was unarmed. "Look . . . Moss . . . I didn't, uh, I didn't . . ."

"Interesting that you know who I am now," Joe said. "Earlier today, you didn't know nothing. Or claimed you didn't. But you knew enough to hire those damn fool pork eaters t' kill me. Gonna pay each of them a hundred dollars, they said. Told them I'd be passed out drunk an' it'd be easy t' take my scalp." Joe held up the two fresh scalps for Tuttle to see. "Wasn't quite that easy, James. Turns out they're the ones as has gone under."

Joe returned the scalps to his war bag and took up the bowie again.

"The thing is, James, I figure t' take one more scalp tonight. Something you ought t' know before we set down t' talk. There was one of those Missouri boys lived long enough t' tell me a few things. Then I finished the son of a bitch off." He drew the edge of the bowie over an imaginary throat, then chuckled. "Don't know as I'll be so easy on you though, James. Might kill you Injun style so's it will take you a couple days t' die, wallowing around in pain an' screaming for your mama."

"Don't kill me, Moss. Don't. Please."

"I can't think of any reason why I shouldn't, you settin' me up t' die like that."

"I can tell you . . . tell you everything, Moss. Just let me live. Everything." The man was sweating profusely and looked like he might pass out there on his own floor. "Everything."

"I dunno, James. I ain't gonna make no promises. Not yet, I ain't. But I reckon I'll listen to what-all you got t' say. Then I'll decide." He smiled, under the circumstances a very chilling expression, and tapped Tuttle lightly on the chest with the tip of the big knife. "So let's us two set down in those chairs over there an' have us a good talk. After that, we'll see do I still want t' kill you or just leave you alone t' fester in your own pus. Go on. Set. An' James . . . one thing more. Any time you decide you want t' make a try for me, why, you just go right ahead." The smile turned into a wickedly mocking grin. "*Any* time, you cocksucking son of a whore."

The insult brought no reaction from the thoroughly terrified trader.

✢ 47 ✢

"H E S-S-SAID HIS name was Holt. Rance Holt. Said he was f-from Nevada. Worked for a man named Peabody. Said he w-was tracking a murderer. Said there's a bounty. The descrip . . ." Tuttle paused to take a deep breath and swallow. "The description fit you to a T. Wanted you. And a woman, too. Handsome woman, he said. Red hair. Traveling with you. Said you was riding a spotted horse. I didn't . . . didn't see a woman nor your horse, but I knew right off it was you he wanted.

"I asked about you. Couple men told me who you are. They said you can handle . . ." Tuttle stopped and rolled his eyes. He shook his head and tried to swallow back the lump of raw fear in his throat. "Said you could handle yourself. I'm no fighter. That's why . . . why I hired those men. To do what I couldn't."

"They couldn't neither, James. That's why they're laying dead out there an' I got their scalps here in my bag."

Joe leaned down closer so that his face loomed over Tuttle's from only a scant few inches away. "It's why I figure t' put your useless scalp in here, too. Now tell me about this sonuvabitch Holt. Where is he now?"

"I don't . . . *south*. Don't *do* that. Please." Tuttle's voice rose into a high-pitched yelp when he felt the tip of Joe's knife lightly tickle his rib cage. One thrust there and he would be a dead man. "Please."

"Where is Holt, James?"

"Julesburg. Maybe Julesburg. Or Denver City."

"I heard of Julesburg, but where is Denver City?"

"It used to be called Cherry Creek."

"All right. Go on."

"He said . . . he said if I k-k . . . got you, I could find him in Manitou, wherever that is."

"I know Manitou," Joe told him. "What else?"

"He said . . . he said . . . oh, God, do I have to tell you this?"

"Yeah. You do." Joe nudged the man with the bowie again and Tuttle tried to flinch away. Joe yanked him back and pressed him back against the counter in his store. The place smelled of wood smoke and fur . . . and fear. Tuttle was sweating even though the inside of the trading post was chilly at this hour. "What did Holt tell you t' do, James?"

"He said I was to . . . to . . . oh, Jesus!"

"Tell me, James." Joe's voice fell to little more than a whisper, but it had a sharper edge to it than his bowie did. It carried the sure promise of death, slow and agonizing death. "Tell me."

"He said I should . . . I should cut . . . cut the head . . . off the man who came here . . . and p-pack it in alcohol . . . in a keg . . . and send it to him at . . . at Manitou. And he could come p-p-pay me f-for . . . p-pay me two thousand dollars re . . . reward."

"Uh-huh. And how much did he give you to bind the deal, James?"

"He didn't . . ." Tuttle looked into Joe's face and saw death looking back at him there. "Five hundred dollars. That's what . . . I gave some of it to those fellows from Indiana. I promised to give them more when . . . you know."

"Yeah. I know. Indiana?"

"Someplace like that. They said they were afraid they were going to be conscripted into Mr. Lincoln's army. They didn't want to go. That's why they . . ." The trader shrugged. "They were going to California."

"They should've kept going," Joe said. "You should've gone with them. Exactly where in Manitou were you t' send this keg of alcohol, James?"

"I have it written down so I wouldn't forget. I . . . I can get it for you. If you, um . . ." He motioned with his hand, asking Joe to back away and let him move away from the counter.

"Sure. Go ahead an' get it." Joe stepped back a pace. Then another.

Tuttle bobbed his head and wiped the cold sweat out of his eyes. The man went behind his store counter and bent low.

When he stood upright again, he had a pistol in his hand. An old-fashioned but very effective—and very deadly—horse pistol. The bore looked big enough to walk into and hardly have to bend over.

It was pointed straight at Joe Moss's chest.

✣ 48 ✣

"YOU STUPID SONUVABITCH," Joe said with a snort of amusement. "If you're gonna kill a man, you should at least ought t' cock your damn pistol."

Tuttle's already pasty face turned white as a sheet of paper, and he looked down at his big pistol.

A moment later, shock turning to anger, he looked up again. "Damn you," he snapped, "this gun already *is* coc—"

Realization came a split second too late. Joe's bowie was already flashing through the air. The distance between the two men was not quite far enough to allow the rotation of the knife to end up point-first in Tuttle's flesh. Instead, the knife struck with the blade flat against the man's chest.

The bowie did no real damage, but it startled Tuttle into flinching. His hand clenched reflexively around the butt of the old dragoon horse pistol. The gun went off, its heavy lead ball flying somewhere into the eaves of the trading post.

Smoke from the discharge of so much gunpowder left

the air in the low-ceilinged trading post reeking of sulphur, and for several long moments obscured vision in that end of the building.

When the smoke began to dissipate, Joe was behind the counter, kneeling on James Tuttle's chest. Joe had retrieved the bowie and was holding it to the man's throat.

"Don't . . . don't . . . please don't hurt me," Tuttle pleaded.

"James, you are fixin' to find out just how much pain a man can live through. An' then I'm gonna let you die."

"No, I . . . I'll tell you . . . everything. Do you hear me, Moss? I can help you. I'll tell you everything you want to know."

A wicked imitation of a grin thinned Joe's lips, and very, very softly he said, "Oh, James, m'lad, I *know* you'll tell me everything I want t' know. There ain't a doubt in the world 'bout that, old son."

Joe snorted. His grin grew even wider. "No, sir," he said as he slid the tip of the bowie into James Tuttle's left nostril, "not a doubt in this whole damn world."

It was the better part of an hour later when Joe emerged from the trading post. A lovely crimson and purple dawn was breaking to the east. The air was crisp and cold, and Joe was feeling pretty good under the circumstances. He still did not know where Fiona was. But he knew where to find Ransom Holt.

He was wearing buckskins again, taken from the trading post stock. His "civilian" clothes were ruined, soaked in blood. He had left them in a sodden pile in a corner of the place. Tuttle he had left in a different sort of pile.

The man had died badly, screaming into an empty nail keg that Joe had slipped over his head to keep his noise from rousing others in the sleeping outpost.

But before he died, he told everything he knew to Joe. Hell, Joe thought, Tuttle probably told him some things the miserable sonuvabitch did not know, too. Made-up things that he desperately hoped would make Joe hurry up and kill him, anything to make the pain stop.

The lies could be sorted out later, Joe figured. The one true fact that he really needed was the information about where to find Holt.

Stopping Holt was the key to making Fiona safe.

Stopping Holt. And then ending this blood feud with whatever Peabodys were left back in Nevada.

Once he'd reached Fort Laramie and had some time to think about his and Fiona's situation instead of concentrating on scurrying about searching for her, Joe realized that if they so desired, the Peabodys could afford to send out a hundred more just like Ransom Holt.

Killing Holt would solve his and Fiona's immediate problem. But it would take killing the source of that trouble to really give them any peace.

One thing he knew for certain. He had to protect Fiona and little Jessica. Protecting them was even more important than reuniting with them, and if he had to choose between knowing they were safe and happy but apart from him, and having them close but being in danger—there was no question what he would unhesitatingly choose. Fiona's and Jessica's safety was far more important than his own.

Joe returned to the corral where his animals were penned. He gave a soft, shrill whistle, and the huge Shire raised its head and whinnied in recognition. The mule, on the other hand, slipped quietly around behind the Shire as if hoping no one would notice it there.

Joe led them outside the corral and tied them to a fence rail, then saddled the patient black horse. When he was done with that, he began the much more complicated task of building a pack for the mule to carry.

At one point when he was nearly ready to ride out from Laramie, he paused and realized with something of a shock that he had been whistling again. But a tune this time. He could not remember what the tune was called, nor could he think of the words, but he remembered the rhythm of it and that was enough.

He had not felt like whistling tunes since . . . since Fiona was with him.

Joe untied his animals, picked up his Henry rifle, and climbed onto the big Shire.

"Come along, boys," he said softly. "We got us some ground t' cover."

✛ 49 ✛

CHERRY CREEK USED to be a pretty decent little run of water. Not worth a damn for beaver, though. Joe knew. He had tried trapping it years ago. Hadn't taken any plews worth spit. Then some damned fool came along and found a little gold, and the rush had been on. Cherry Creek, Georgetown, there was a whole string of brand-new gold camps growing like mushrooms along the headwaters of the South Platte and its many tributaries.

Joe scowled. Some of those creeks provided a fair catch of beaver. Now they were being ruined. And yes, he knew good and well—too damned well—that beaver wasn't worth much these days. Still and all, he hated to see good country ruined with the presence of pork eaters who did not know how to make a trap set and had never seen a hostile Indian. Assholes! Joe had had a bellyful of them.

On the other hand, he thought, his expression lightening, wherever there were gold miners there was whiskey.

And he had not gotten all the whiskey he wanted back at Fort Laramie.

Denver City, as they were calling it now, smelled of smoke from all the supper fires that were burning in all those buildings. Joe shook his head. There must have been five thousand people here now. Maybe more.

It took him a moment to realize what was wrong about the scents in the air. Coal. It was coal smoke he was smelling, not wood. Somebody must have started digging coal around here; they surely could not haul it all the way out from back East. The country was coming to ruination for certain sure if women were here cooking with coal.

That stink was not enough to keep him out of the first saloon he came to.

He had to ride two more blocks to find a livery stable that was clean and had a hostler who looked trustworthy.

"Evenin', friend," Joe said as he dismounted and led his animals into the barn alleyway.

"Evenin' your own self," the young man said, rising off the rat-proof grain bunk where he had been perched. "What can I do for you?"

"I got a powerful thirst on me, son, and I want t' make sure my critters are safe an' tended to while I'm about the business o' satisfying that thirst."

"I can assure you they would be safe here. Your trappings, too, if you like. Put the animals in the second stall on that side there. You can pile your gear inside the tack room there. I sleep in there and won't nobody come in and bother your things during the night."

Joe nodded and reached into his possibles pouch. "You want I should pay you now?" He grinned and added, "Just in case there's none o' this left by the time I get back?"

The young hostler laughed. "I know what you mean. Sure. I charge fifty cents per night per animal." He looked at the huge Shire and said, "Maybe I should raise my rate for that one, though."

"What you think is fair," Joe said.

"No, no, I won't be asking extra for him. Why, I count it a privilege to have a fine animal like that staying in my place. He's a Shire, isn't he?"

"So said the man I bought him off of."

"Did he come all the way from England, then?"

Joe could only shrug. "The man didn't say."

"My, my, he is a beauty. Look at those feet. He must take five pounds of iron in every shoe. How are his shoes, by the way?"

"Fair. Big as he is, he wears on them fast."

"Would you like me to shoe him while you're here? I'd love a chance to work on something like him."

"How much?" It crossed Joe's mind that this young man might be making a show of fairness with one hand so he could inflate his prices with the other.

"Twenty-five cents a foot," the young fellow said. That price was more than fair, it was generous. Twice that would have been fair, and Joe was more or less expecting a dollar a hoof or something equally outlandish.

Joe pulled out some cash. "I'll pay you to shoe both animals, then, and board them two nights."

The hostler looked down at the currency in Joe's hand and quickly shook his head. "Sorry."

"What's the matter?" Joe asked.

"I'm sorry, friend, but I don't take paper money. Hard money only."

"What the hell is that about?"

"Friend, it's obvious that you're new here. You might say that Denver is a border town. There are Unionists to the north of us and Confederates to the south. Right here we have both. Try to spend paper money, and you're apt to offend by giving Union paper to a Reb or offering Confed'rate money to a Yank. Feelings on the subject tend to run hot. Most merchants avoid conflict by dealing in hard money only, gold and silver being sound regardless of who minted the coins."

Joe shook his head. "Where I been, son, I tend t' forget there is such a thing as a war back East. I got a little hard money on me, but not much. Is there anyplace I can exchange paper for coin?"

"The banks will take Union currency and exchange it almost straight up. Some of the hotels will let you buy coin from them, but you have to pay a premium, a little if you're holding Yankee money but a lot if your paper is Confederate."

Joe dug deeper into his pouch and came up with a ten-dollar eagle. Handing it to the hostler, he said, "This will keep my boys for a few days. Now please point me to one o' them hotels that will change soft money for hard."

The young fellow walked to the front of his barn, and only then did Joe see that he was crippled, his right leg twisted and shorter than the left. "Down there on the left. The Weymouth, it's called. I've never stayed there myself, but I've heard the rooms are cleaner than most."

"All right. Thanks a lot." Joe carried his gear into the tack room and piled everything in a corner where it should be out of the way, then picked up his bedroll—more out of habit than necessity—and headed down the street to the Weymouth Hotel.

He was looking forward to a bath and a real bed. And even more to a few mugs of whiskey.

Another day or maybe two should take him to Manitou, he calculated, and a showdown with Ransom Holt.

✣ 50 ✣

"I NEED A ROOM for a night or two an' I don't want to share the bed," he told the graybeard at the Weymouth's desk.

"Huh. I wisht we had enough business to be packing them in two or three to the bed. We used to, you know, back when we first opened. Not no more, though. It's two dollars a night. In advance." He pushed a canvas-bound ledger at Joe. "Make your mark here."

Joe chose a pen with a narrow nib and dipped it in the inkwell, then signed his name. He still experienced a flush of pride and pleasure whenever he did that. He could by damn read now and write, too. Not just everybody could do that.

"Room Three. Top of the stairs, Mister, uh"—the old fellow turned the ledger around and peered at the signature—"Mr. Moss."

"Is there a key?"

"Nope. The locks was cheap pieces of shit to begin with and they're every one busted now. If you have any valuables, you can leave them with me. I got a safe in my room there if you want to use it."

Joe shook his head. Anything of any value was over at the livery. His bedroll included his camp bed and a change of clean socks and underwear and that was about it. "No need, thanks. How 'bout a bath?"

"Just around the corner there's a barbershop that has a tub."

Joe nodded and felt his face and the back of his head. He hadn't taken time for a haircut in a spell. It might make a nice change to let someone else cut it. A trim off the beard, too, while he was at it. He smiled and thanked the man, then paid the fellow five dollars in U.S. currency.

"One night?"

"Could be two. You can give me my change when I leave."

"That's fair," the clerk said.

Joe tramped up the stairs and looked around Room Three. Not that there was much to see. There was a rope-sprung bed with a thin mattress and two aged blankets. A series of pegs on one wall for hanging clothes. And that was about it.

The floorboards squeaked when he walked across them. Joe liked that. It meant no one could approach in the night without alerting him.

He dropped his bedroll on the foot of the bed and immediately turned back around and left, the Henry still trailing from his hand. He did not intend to leave the repeater unattended. There was no sign of the desk clerk when he went downstairs. Joe went outside and turned in the direction the man had pointed for that barbershop. A bath was going to feel good.

Joe paused, though, outside the open doorway to one of Denver's many saloons. A bath would feel good, but it would feel even better if he had a drink in his belly to warm his innards first.

And the aromas coming out of the place . . . beer and whiskey and cigar smoke . . . were purely tantalizing.

Yeah, the bath could wait just a little.

"Beer for you, mister?" the barman asked.

"Whiskey," Joe answered, leaning the Henry against the front of the bar. He dug into his pouch for another piece of paper currency, a twenty. He hadn't gotten around yet to exchanging his paper money for coin. Tomorrow maybe.

The barman eyed the bill, then said, "A drink costs more if you don't have hard money."

"How much?"

"Fifty cents."

The price was outrageous, but Joe nodded acceptance of the highway robbery.

The barman made change with a mixture of coins and paper, then poured a generous tot of bar whiskey into a mug. The place did not skimp on its measure.

Joe checked to see that there was no Confederate money mixed into his change, then tried the whiskey. It was the real thing, not Injun whiskey, smooth on the tongue and fiery in the gut. He had a second swallow, then set the mug back onto the bar before turning sideways to the bar and propping an elbow next to his drink.

He liked the place. It did not pretend to be anything but a place for a man to have a drink and relax. There were no wheels or faro or dice. No piano or dancing girls. Not even any whores.

There were a good many men in the place, most of them in the rough clothes of working men with not a batwing collar or a boiled shirt among them.

Blood at Bear Lake

A large man with a black beard and whiskey-flushed cheeks stopped beside Joe. "Is that one of them newfangled Henry rifles?"

Joe nodded. "Aye, so 'tis."

"Can I pick it up and feel the heft of it?"

"Sorry. No," Joe said. "I don't let anybody handle my weapons."

"I been thinking about trying to buy me one of those," the bear of a man said.

"You won't be sorry if you get one," Joe said, then pointedly turned to face the counter, giving his shoulder to the fellow. He picked up his mug and had another very small sip of the whiskey. Like all whiskey, it was getting better-tasting the more he had of it.

"I just want to touch it. I ain't gonna run off with it." The fellow's voice was rising and taking a hard edge.

Joe craned his head around and looked the fellow up and down. The increasingly belligerent fellow did not seem to be armed. Joe looked him over, then turned back to the bar.

There was a piece of polished steel on the back wall instead of a mirror. It was sufficiently reflective that Joe could keep an eye on this gent while ignoring him.

It was a shame, but the thought of a second whiskey was becoming less and less attractive.

Joe raised his mug again. A couple more swallows would finish this drink; then he could go get his bath.

The big man reached in front of Joe and wrapped his hand around the barrel of the Henry.

Damn, Joe thought. Just damn it all to hell anyway.

He whirled, his elbow slamming into the fellow's face. There was a satisfying crunch of breaking cartilage, and blood sprayed for four or five feet around.

The man's eyes went wide. He tottered backward two paces and shook his head like an old buffalo bull that is already dead on its feet but does not yet know it. Then the fellow threw his head back and roared.

That sounded like a bull, too, Joe thought. A little.

The fellow lowered his head and charged straight ahead.

51

JOE STEPPED AWAY a pace and took a sharp, backhand swing with the Henry. The octagon steel barrel caught the fellow across the face and caved in his cheekbone.

The man cried out. But he did not quit. He blindly reached for Joe with one hand while he wiped blood out of his eyes with the other.

Joe rather admired the son of a bitch's grit. But not so much that he was willing to let the fellow put hands on him. Instead, Joe took another step backward and brought the butt of the Henry up into the tough son of a bitch's nuts.

There was no outcry this time. The guy simply folded up and collapsed. Passed out cold as a trout.

"Mister, you'd best not be here when Dinkin comes to. He's the meanest sonuvabitch in the territory."

Joe picked up his whiskey and drained it. "Was maybe," he said. He wiped his mouth with the back of his hand, nodded a friendly enough farewell to the gents who were standing around gawking, then took the gentleman's advice and left. He still wanted that bath, after all. Make that *needed*.

Off to the west, the sun had already slipped below the mountain peaks, and there was a decided chill in the air, but the barbershop was still open. There were a couple gents inside playing some sort of game on what looked like a checkerboard but with different-shaped pieces. One of those fellows turned out to be the barber.

"Yes, sir. What can I do for you?"

"I'm needin' a bath. A trim might not go too bad since I'm already here."

"Sit in the chair there. I'll be with you soon as I make this next move." He did something with one of the pieces on his board, and the other gent scowled. Judging from that, Joe would have to figure that the barber was winning.

Joe propped the Henry against the wall and settled into the chair, a proper barber chair that lay back or swung around in circles and was bolted to the floor.

Joe had not seen a chair like that in a very long time. In San Francisco, would that have been? Or Santa Fe? He was not sure, but it had been years back. He was positive about that much.

"Do you want a shave?" the barber asked. "Or just a trim?"

"Just the trim, thanks. Shave it off an' it'll just itch me half t' death when it starts growin' back in again."

"A trim it will be, then."

The barber threw a striped sheet over him and snugged it tight around his neck, then took up his shears and began snipping. A few minutes later, Joe's shaggy mane had been chopped down to a manageable length and he felt five pounds lighter.

"Now for that bath," he said when the barber took the sheet off him, curls of dark hair mixed with gray falling to the floor when he did so.

"Through that door there. Got a row of stalls back there. Pick any one you like and step in. My China boy will pour water into the bucket overhead. Bucket's got little holes in the bottom so the water runs over you when you stand under it. It works good and you never have to be sitting in water that has the last fellow's dirt in it."

"I think I like that idea," Joe said.

"Most do. Go on now." The barber tugged a cord that led into the ceiling.

"What was that?"

"Bellpull. To tell the Chinaman there's somebody coming." The man handed Joe a large Turkish towel—a real towel and not just some discarded grain sack—and motioned him toward the door.

Joe picked up his Henry and went into the back room, which smelled of soap and moisture. It was lighted by a pair of good lamps mounted high on the walls. There were three narrow stalls, each with a swinging door to give privacy. Fancy, Joe thought.

He peered inside the nearest stall. Sure enough, there was a bucket hanging overhead, and the floor had slats that allowed water draining out of the bucket to drain away somewhere. There was a hook bolted to the back of the door where a man could hang things, the towels perhaps, and a metal dish of pale, runny soap on the back wall.

He could not see behind the stalls, but apparently there was some sort of platform or ramp back there because he could see some shiny black hair and a pair of slanted eyes peeping over the back wall. The Chinaman, he assumed, stationed where he could reach over to pour the water. Joe smiled and waved and the eyes quickly disappeared.

Joe went down to the last stall and looked inside, then leaned his rifle in a corner just outside the door to that stall. He sat on the bench that ran along the side of the room and removed his boots—when he had time to think about such things he wanted to find some moccasins instead, maybe find himself a squaw who could make him some because he doubted that Fiona would know how—and piled his clothing and accoutrements on the bench. He placed his revolver and bowie on top of the pile, then stepped into the bath stall.

He heard a faint rustling noise from behind the back wall and saw the Chinaman—he was a wiry little son of a bitch and wore his hair in a pigtail—lean over and dump a pail of water into the overhead bucket.

Immediately, thin streams of water, *warm* water, began streaming down all over him. It was like a very warm summer rain. Joe liked it.

He took a fingerful of soft soap from the metal dish that was screwed onto the wall and began to wash himself.

Now, this was some kind of all right! Maybe, he conceded, there was something to be said for fancified city notions after all.

While he lathered himself up, he began softly humming a Lakota chant.

Then he heard the door to the back room open and the approach of heavy footsteps. A moment later, a deep voice growled, "All my life I heard the expression 'caught with his pants down.' Now I see it can happen for true." The voice laughed. "Come out, Moss. See if you can make it to your guns before I cut you down."

Joe heard the Chinaman scurry away.

Blood at Bear Lake

All of a sudden, the warmth inside the bath stall evaporated, and Joe felt a chill rise up out of nowhere to make his skin prickle with goose bumps.

"Come out of there, you son of a bitch."

52

"DINKIN?"
    "What the fuck is dinkin?" the voice returned.

All right. This was not the fellow Joe had busted up in the saloon. And he knew Joe's name, which meant he likely was one of Ransom Holt's assassins, damn him.

"You kinda caught me at a bad time here," Joe said. "Can we talk about this?"

"Hell, no, we can't. And you ain't climbing out over that back wall neither. I get my bath here lots and I know how the place is laid out. If you try and climb over, I can see you and shoot your hairy ass. Might have to take a head shot, though, and that would piss me off. It'd be messy, and I got to have your head to deliver to the man."

"Give me a minute to wipe the soap outa my eyes an' I'll come out," Joe said.

"Go ahead. But don't think you're gonna camp there too

awful long. Come out and try for one of these guns whenever you're ready."

"You've already took my guns, ain't you?"

"Have I? Come out and see," the fellow taunted.

"D'you mind if I know your name?" Joe asked.

"When you get to Hell and the devil asks what happened, you can tell the son of a bitch that James Drew killed you and collected the bounty."

While the two were talking through the thin wood of the bath stall door, Joe was carefully assessing where James Drew was standing. Once he was sure of that, he silently slipped the hook free so the door could swing freely open.

He took a deep breath and, with a roar, used his left hand to slap the door open. He stepped confidently out of the stall. He had the bath towel wrapped around his waist.

And he had his tomahawk in his right hand.

James Drew's revolver spat flame, and a wreath of white smoke blossomed from the muzzle. Joe felt a hard thump low on his right side.

He was hit. He did not know how badly, but he could not take time to worry about it. Not now. First he had to . . .

He gauged the distance and stepped back a pace while Drew's thumb hooked over the hammer and started to draw it back for a second shot.

The man did not have time enough for that. Joe's tomahawk flashed, turning end over end toward Drew.

The hired gunman flinched away from the spinning 'hawk, trying to bat it aside with the barrel of his revolver. The gun discharged harmlessly to one side while the tomahawk buried itself in Drew's shoulder.

Drew looked up in time to see Joe Moss flying toward him. Slamming into him with a snarl of rage. Driving him backward onto the bench that ran along the wall.

Joe's knee found Drew's cods, and Drew shrieked.

Drew was a wiry sonuvabitch who looked like he had been in a fight or two in his past, but he had never fought with Joe Moss, probably not with any of Joe's mountain man companions either. Mountain men were accustomed to rough-and-tumble. They fought like this for sport. And sometimes for survival.

Joe took a handful of Drew's black, greasy hair and used it as a handle so he could drive the man's head repeatedly against the barbershop wall.

"Quit. Please. I . . . I yield. I give. You win," Drew grunted desperately as consciousness began to slip away.

"Damn right I win," Joe snarled. He stopped pounding Drew's head against the wall and sat up. Without changing expression, he took the shaft of the tomahawk and with a jerk and a twist yanked it free of Drew's flesh.

"Thanks," Drew mumbled. "Thank you . . . for that."

"Oh, don't thank me yet," Joe said.

Then, smiling, he drove the blade of his 'hawk square into the middle of James Drew's forehead. The man's body stiffened, quivered just a little, and then deflated.

With a grunt, Joe stood and jerked his tomahawk free of James Drew's brain. Then he turned and began gathering his other weapons and clothing.

He surely did feel better after that bath.

✛ 53 ✛

AFTER JOE DRESSED and had all his weapons in their proper places, he sat on the bench beside James Drew's corpse and cut a scrap of cloth off Drew's shirttail. Then he began meticulously cleaning the greasy brain matter and drying blood off the tomahawk.

His movements were slow and methodical. His thoughts were anything but.

Drew was a total stranger. So had been James Tuttle back at Fort Laramie. Yet both had tried to kill him. They wanted the Peabody reward money and were willing to take a life to get it. Take a life and deliver the head.

Dammit, they could come at Fiona just as savagely. Cut her beautiful head from her body and take it to Ransom Holt. And he, the son of a bitch, would send it on to whichever of the Peabodys was still alive. Damn them all!

It occurred to Joe that pickling salts discolor anything

placed in them. He might take the hounds off Fiona's trail by sending Ransom Holt a woman's head.

Not Fiona's, of course. But he could rob a grave. If he could find a young woman freshly dead. But dammit, even if he could do that, how in hell could he find one with red hair? That flaming hair was Fiona's most distinguishing characteristic. It was mighty unlikely that he could find a freshly dead female to decapitate.

He would not hesitate, not for a heartbeat, if he could do that.

Take the already dead woman's head—he was no murderer, dammit, no matter how many men and, yes, women, too, he had killed—and send it to Holt.

He chuckled. He could even collect the bounty Holt was offering on Fiona. Now, wouldn't that be a kick in the teeth for the Peabodys?

With a sigh, Joe slipped the tomahawk back into his sash where it belonged. He was just daydreaming, dammit, and dreams won't come to beaver.

Joe had been looking forward to a little rest here in Denver. But while he was lollygagging around with a bath and a haircut, there were men out there in the night who were actively looking for his own dear Fiona. And they would most cruelly handle her if ever they caught up with her and that little chestnut horse.

Piss on this, Joe decided.

He could rest when Fiona was safe. And he knew the best way to make that so.

Joe stepped out into the barber's front room and hooked a thumb over his shoulder. "That fella you sent back there t' get me got got his own self. You might wanta drag him out of there before your bath customers start complaining 'bout the stink."

"Stink?" the startled barber repeated.

Blood at Bear Lake

"Aye. The man shit his britches when I kill't him." Joe shook his head. "Had no sense o' decorum a'tall."

He dropped a quarter into the barber's tip plate to help pay for the removal and burying, then headed at a fast walk for the hotel where he had left his bedroll.

He could think about sleep later.

Fiona needed him *now*.

✢ 54 ✢

JOE PUSHED THE big Shire hard, dragging the recalcitrant little mule along behind. He hit the headwaters of Fountain Creek well before dawn and followed it south.

He had been on Fountain many a time in other, older days, back when there was nothing but buffalo and mule deer to be found on the rolling hills that lay beneath the Front Range. Game, that is, and Indians, not all of whom were friendly.

Back then, the only outposts of civilization had been Pueblo all the way south to the Arkansas and Bent's Fort well east in the Arkansas Valley.

Those were damned fine days, Joe thought. Damn fine.

Now there was a town called Fountain and another at the mystical springs at Manitou. Lord knows where-all else the emigrants might be making towns for themselves.

Not that Joe was complaining. He accepted the fact that

the days of beaver and the free trapper were past. He accepted it. But he hated it nonetheless.

He pushed the Shire until the white foam of sweat mottled the shiny black of its hide, and dawn found him close to the foothills below the wall of magnificent mountains, nearing the place where Four Mile Creek flowed into Fountain Creek. Close, too, to the young town of Fountain, close enough that he could see the smoke from folks' chimneys there.

Joe angled west, cut across some hills, and encountered a road. Damn thing hadn't been there the last time he came this way, but there was a right proper road in place now. It even had some bridges and culverts to ease the way for wagon traffic.

"What d'you make of a thing like that, horse?" he asked, shaking his head. A road. Be damned if it wasn't.

Why, there was even a town of sorts there, too. He didn't know what it was called and did not particularly want to know. Ransom Holt was supposed to be in Manitou, and that was still a couple miles west, smack at the foot of the pass the Utes took each year on their migrations from the mountain wintering grounds to the vast plains where they spent their summers hunting.

Lordy, but this country did bring back memories.

Joe always got along well with the Utes—something not just everyone could say—and had hunted with them a number of times in the past.

He called to mind one wonderful winter spent in South Park, living with a fat Ute girl who surely did know how to drain a man's seed. The beaver were prime and the elk tasty, and what more could a man ask than that?

If he could do something like that with Fiona, find a high mountain hideaway and come down only once a year to swap hides for salt, tobacco, and gunpowder . . . Joe shook himself out of his what-if reverie. He hadn't come here to daydream, dammit.

He was here to kill a man.

Colorado City, that was the name he saw on a couple of the businesses he rode past on his way through the young town. Not that there was so very much to be called a town. Just a few structures, most of them hastily constructed and with canvas for roofs.

There were a few who built with brick and with stone, though, so somebody hereabouts intended to stay.

Joe rode on past. When he left Colorado City, he reined the Shire off the road into a small grove of aspen. The big horse was played out. Its legs were trembling and its coat quivered when he touched it.

"It's all right, little fella. You've done everything I asked of you. You've earned yourself a rest."

Joe took the reins in hand and led his animals the last mile to Manitou.

The little town was in nearly perpetual shadow, set as it was in a wide cleft that cut into the mountains. Ute Pass ran west from Manitou, the mountains there dominated by the ever-white cap atop the mountain they were now calling Pikes Peak in honor of old Zebulon. Ute Pass entered the mountains just to the north of the peak.

Joe's concentration right now, though, was on Manitou. And the man Ransom Holt who'd put a price on his head and on Fiona's.

It was well past daybreak now, getting on toward the middle of the morning, and he had pushed the Shire hard since just past sundown yesterday. The horse deserved to be taken care of before Joe was.

He spotted a stable on his right. A sign offered to board

horses for ten cents a day. It was a good price, but then wild grass hay should be easily come by here. Just take a mower and a rake out onto the plains, and a man could cut all the hay he wanted with no one to tell him nay.

"I got me some tired animals here, friend," Joe told the hostler who came to greet him. "They need hay and a good rubdown. Water after they've cooled off. Can you do those things for me? I'm willin' to pay."

The hostler, a middle-aged man who was badly in need of a shave and a haircut, scratched his chin and nodded. "If you say you'll pay extra."

"I say it," Joe affirmed.

"Going to be here long?"

"Don't know yet," Joe told him. Maybe forever, he thought, but he did not say that.

"Throw your things over there until you decide," the hostler said. "I'll take good care of these tired boys."

Joe thanked the man and shucked the Henry from his scabbard before leaving the animals in the care of the hostler.

Ransom Holt was supposed to be at a hotel called the Simcox House. Joe intended to find the man and to shoot the son of a bitch on sight just as sure as he would shoot down a hydrophobic dog. No questions; no hesitation.

✛ 55 ✛

THERE WERE NO buildings in Manitou that could be considered to be "old," but the Simcox House was closer to it than most. Why, it had been in place long enough for the paint on the windowsills to peel. Joe mounted the steps to the front porch and looked behind him.

The hotel was on a hillside, looking down on the little town that snaked along the course of the creek that descended from the Front Range mountains. Joe could see pretty much the whole of the town. But what he truly wanted to see was Ransom Holt. Or his own beloved Fiona.

With a grunt of determination, Joe Moss squared his shoulders, placed the Henry in the crook of his left arm, and entered the Simcox House.

The lobby was dark, filled with heavy furniture and stuffed elk heads. Cuspidors were placed conveniently among the chairs, and there were ashtrays provided for the cigar smokers. If the place was busy, it did not show it. One gentleman sat in a deep upholstered armchair with a newspaper spread in his lap, and there was a young man with slicked-down hair and sleeve garters fiddling with sheaves of papers at a small desk toward the rear of the lobby.

"May I help you?" the youngster with the sleeve garters asked.

Joe strode across the Oriental rugs on the lobby floor and grounded the butt of his Henry. "Ayuh. I'm lookin' for a fella that I'm told should be here. Man name of Holt. Ransom Holt."

The young clerk smiled. "Mr. Holt. Yes, we've had the privilege of his business. But he isn't here any longer."

"Not here?" Joe blurted. "I don't understand."

"You missed him by just two days," the clerk said. "He left the day before yesterday."

"Where'd he go, man? This is real important."

"Oh, I wouldn't know where he went when he left here. I only know he left in something of a hurry. He left most of his things. Said he would be back for them later or send for them if he couldn't return."

"An' you don't know where he's gone nor when he might be back?" Joe asked.

The young fellow shook his head. "No, I don't. Sorry."

"Damn," Joe muttered, mostly to himself. Then, in a louder voice, he asked, "You say Mr. Holt was in a hurry when he left. Do you know what caused him to rush away like that?"

"No, of course not. We don't interfere in our guests' lives."

Joe took a twenty-dollar bill out of his pouch and laid it on the clerk's desk. The young man looked up, clearly startled. His eyes darted left and right. Then the twenty disappeared.

He cleared his throat and rather nervously glanced around the room again before he spoke. "All I know, and I mean it's all I know, is that Mr. Holt received a telegraphic message. The boy delivered it when Mr. Holt was at breakfast. He left his table immediately, went upstairs, and came back down a few minutes later carrying a hand valise."

"Two days. Damn." Joe turned to leave, then thought of something else that might be of value. He turned back to the clerk. "Does Holt keep his own horse or does he use public transportation?"

"The gentleman went from here to the stage depot. I did notice that much."

Joe pursed his lips and thought for a moment, then said, "All right, kid, thanks. You been a big help."

He turned and headed toward the door. Stopped. Turned back again. "Where could I find the telegraph office hereabouts?"

"Just down the street, sir. Next door to the bank. You can't miss it."

Joe smiled and thanked him again, then hurried on his way.

Two days gone. Damn that son of a bitch!

56

"EXCUSE ME, SIR," Joe said. "I need some information."
     The telegrapher, a young fellow with blond hair falling over his eyes, looked up and smiled a welcome. "Yes, of course. What do you need to know?"

"Two days ago, a fella over at the Simcox House received a message. I need t' know where it came from an' what it said."

"Oh, sir, I am sure you understand that I cannot possibly give you that information." The smile returned. "It would be against all the rules. Really."

"Friend, this is awful important t' me. I really got t' know. Really." Joe was not smiling.

"But our rules prohibit it."

"Prohibit," Joe repeated. "That means no, don't it?"

"More or less."

"I tell ya what. Maybe this would help." Joe dipped into his possibles pouch and laid a sheaf of twenty-dollar bills on the counter. He did not bother to count them, but the amount should have been in the neighborhood of a hundred dollars.

"Oh, sir. I can't take your money. Believe me, I would like to. But I cannot."

"I told you it's important, son. My wife's life might could depend on it," Joe said, leaning on the counter. Seriousness and urgency were written plain on his face. "An' I ain't just sayin' that. Her actual life is at stake here."

"I appreciate the seriousness, sir, but the rules are very specific. People have the right to expect privacy in their wires, just as in their letters. I simply cannot do it."

Joe sighed. "You won't take that money, son?"

"No, sir. I will not."

Slowly and carefully, Joe picked up the currency, folded and sorted it, then returned it to his possibles pouch. "I sure wisht I could change your mind, sonny."

"Sorry. That's not possible."

"Okay. But remember that I tried."

Joe turned and walked to the door, but instead of leaving the telegraph office, he pulled the blind down to cover the window, set the CLOSED sign there where it could be seen from outside, and twisted the brass lock.

"Sir?" the telegrapher sputtered as Joe set his Henry aside and entered the telegrapher's fenced-off portion of the room. "Sir!" he repeated when the bowie came into Joe's hand.

Joe ignored him for the moment. Ripped one of the sleeves from the youngster's shirt. Wadded the cloth into a ball and shoved it into the young man's mouth.

Then Joe leaned down and, still without rushing, calmly said, "What I am gonna do is slice off pieces o' you till you loosen up an' tell me what it is that I want t' know. Now hold still whilst I tie you in place." A smile flickered briefly across Joe's leathery face. "It wouldn't be polite for you t' wiggle, now would it?"

The telegrapher frantically snatched the gag from his mouth and, pale and sputtering, said, "You . . . you're serious!"

"Aye. I told you. My wife's life could be at stake here. Given the choice, I'd ruther leave your guts in a pile on this floor than t' see a hair on her head come to harm. Now shut up. I figure to start carving. I'll quit when you're ready t' tell me what I need t' know."

Joe grabbed the gag away from the fellow and leaned close.

"No, I . . . I'll tell you. Whatever you . . . whatever you want."

"You took a message for Ransom Holt."

"I'm sure I did, but I don't remember every wire I copy."

"Copy. You keep a copy o' all the messages for your own selves, don't you?"

The telegrapher nodded, his Adam's apple bobbing nervously. "Yes, sir. We do."

"Find it. Show me what it says an' where it came from. Do it right damned now!"

The telegrapher practically flew out of his chair to one of several filing cabinets ranked along the wall.

57

"IT'S A FUNNY thing, mister, but you're the second fellow to ask me that question this week."

"And what did you tell the first man to ask it?" Joe inquired of the stage line ticket agent.

"Same thing I'll tell you. This right here is as far west as the roads run. Not until you get all the way up to the Oregon Trail or south to the Gila Road. From here, the best way across to Utah is to take a coach north to Denver. You change there and connect with another that will carry you east to Julesburg. I can ticket you through that far, but in Julesburg you'll have to make your own arrangements with the Overland Express Company coach on west to Utah. The place you're looking for is supposed to be somewhere up around Bear Lake."

"How would you know that, mister?"

"That other fellow, he had me wire back to the operator who originated the message. I asked him and he told me."

The man shrugged. "I hadn't heard of it until then. Bear Lake, I mean. I'd heard of Utah all right."

"Let me get the straight of it. North to Denver. Back east all the way out to Julesburg. Then roll west from there along the Oregon road. Is that right?"

The ticket agent nodded. "Yes, sir, it is."

"You've been a big help, thanks."

Joe left the stage depot and headed for the livery where he had left his Shire and mule.

The contents of Ransom Holt's telegraph message kept thundering through his mind, banging on the walls of his brain like a skull-crushing mallet.

HAVE WOMAN BRING MONEY
S/CHARLES COMMA BEAR LAKE

Have woman. Bring money.

And Ransom Holt, the son of a bitch, was on his way to deliver it. And to collect Fiona's dear head.

If they had harmed her . . .

Joe put Fiona out of his mind. She would never be out of his heart, but for now he needed to think. He had to find a way to get to Fiona and this Charles person before Holt did.

Bastard Charles did not even say if he had her alive. Or . . . otherwise.

Joe could not be thinking about that now. He simply had to believe that she was alive and that he could find her and free her. She *had* to be.

At the livery, he entered the stall where the huge Shire was stabled with good hay, grain, and clean water. One look told Joe the big horse would not be traveling anywhere for a good many days. It needed time to recover from the hard use Joe had put it to over the past few days.

"You can see I've tooken good care of 'em," the hostler said, coming up behind Joe, carrying a scrap of harness leather.

"Yes, sir, you have, but now I'm needing a fast horse. Better yet, several of them."

"I can show you what I have," the man said. "Follow me back this way."

When they got to the corral at the rear of the livery barn, Joe quickly dismissed the nags that were standing there. They looked like they might make decent cart or plow horses, but they were no mountain ponies and were not going to take anyone anywhere in any sort of a hurry.

"You haven't had somebody else in here looking for a fast horse in the past couple days, have you?" Joe asked.

The hostler have him an odd look. "No, I haven't. Why'd you ask a thing like that?"

Joe shrugged. "Everywhere I go lately, there's somebody else been there just ahead of me."

He meant it, but the hostler took it for a joke and laughed. "Nothing like that, no, sir."

"Shit!" Joe grumbled.

"If you go back up to the springs, you might could catch some Injuns there. They might have spare horses. Might even have some decent horseflesh among 'em. And you know Injuns. Make them the right price and they'll sell anything they got. Including their wives or daughters."

Joe did not necessarily agree with that assessment, not completely anyway, but the man did have a point. "They still camp in that grove up above the springs?"

"You know the area, do you?"

"I do."

"Well, you'll find the Injuns just where you said. Funny how all the different tribes come here, but they don't fight

218

amongst themselves when they do. Why is that, do you wonder?"

"It's because those waters are sacred to the Great Spirit Manitou. It would be an insult to him if they was to hog the spring. Indians are funny that way."

"Whacha mean 'funny'?"

"I mean they respect their gods more than they hate their enemies. That kind of funny." He got the impression that the livery man did not really understand what he meant by that, but in truth Joe did not care. The fellow had given him an idea where he might find the horses he needed. That was what mattered.

"I'll leave my things here if you don't mind," he said. "Might be away for a spell, but I'll be back sooner or later."

"Everything will be here when you come, whenever that is," the hostler said.

Joe left a fistful of U.S. currency with him to take care of the Shire and the mule, then headed toward the Indian campground above the sacred springs.

✢ 58 ✢

THERE WAS A small band of Arapaho camping above the sacred spring.

Joe climbed a pale red gravel slope, then descended into a pine-scented grove where generations of Indians had camped when they made their pilgrimages to the spring.

Now the Arapaho eyed Joe warily as he approached them, probably suspicious all the more because he came on foot.

"No Engliss. No Engliss. Go 'way."

Joe spoke to them in the universal sign language of the plains. "I am Man Killer. You know me."

One of the men, a young man with bulging muscles and a scowl, said, "I am Running Calf. What want you here, Man Killer?"

"My horse is played out. I have many miles to go. I have money to buy a horse from you, Running Calf. Good horse. Mountain horse. I will pay."

"What would we buy with white man's money?"

"Tobacco. Much tobacco. Whiskey."

"We are not permitted to buy whiskey. The whites here will not sell it to us. You know this, Man Killer."

Joe smiled and signed back, "But they will sell to me."

Running Calf smiled as well, and Joe figured he had as good as bought his horse now.

It was not that easy. There were still the painstaking negotiations to complete, and it would have been unwise to try to shortcut the process. As it was, Joe considered himself lucky to get out of there in under two hours.

He had expected that, but was disappointed that the band would sell him only one horse. The group was not traveling with any mounts to spare, and throughout the negotiations complained that two of them would have to ride double because of being a horse short.

Joe knew good and well someone would be riding two to a horse no farther than Manitou. They were sure to steal another horse there. Or likely more than one. Not that it would have been polite to mention that.

On second thought, he realized that the good folks of Manitou were probably safe from horse theft by the Arapaho. The Indians would not want to make themselves unwelcome here lest they all be evicted from the sacred waters.

With a hidden grin, Joe speculated that it would be some good burgher out east in Fountain or maybe Colorado City who would lose his horse. No matter. He needed a horse. He needed it now. And if some pork-eating son of a bitch had to lose his horse so Joe could buy one, so be it.

"Yes," Joe finally signed. "Two kegs. I will leave them there." He pointed. "Under those trees will I leave them."

"And the tobacco, Man Killer?"

"There. Same with the whiskey. I will leave seven twists."

"Ten. Leave ten."

"We agreed on seven. Are you not a man whose word is good?"

There was a stir of unease among the rest of the band, but Running Calf seemed unfazed. "Seven, yes," Running Calf affirmed.

Joe grunted and bobbed his head, then brought out tobacco and offered it all around before filling his pipe. Running Calf pushed a twig into the fire, then held it for Joe to ignite the tobacco.

The horse looked like a good one. Joe figured to use it hard.

He would be riding Indian style, with just a blanket instead of a saddle. No stirrups. No bridle, just a single rein tied around the gaudy paint's jaw. And no more gear than he could carry draped on his own person.

"I will get the whiskey and the tobacco, then collect my horse," he signed.

"Let it be so."

Joe's knees popped like Chinese firecrackers when he stood after squatting so long. He turned and headed back toward Manitou.

RIDING BAREBACK SAVE for a blanket folded and thrown over the animal's back, and with his Henry rifle balanced across his lap, Joe put the paint horse into a lope and held it at that gait up the twisting, tortuous climb toward vast South Park, the Bayou Salado.

He passed magnificent rock formations, stands of dark timber where majestic elk lurked, and expanses of grass that was belly deep. He pushed the horse hard as miles and miles fell behind.

At the top of the pass, he urged the paint even harder. He was killing it. He knew that he was. But Fiona . . . Fiona. He would gladly slaughter this and a thousand horses more to save one drop of her precious blood.

Joe pressed the horse hard, barely allowing it rest, throughout the day and into the night.

At night at that elevation, the cold was bitter and he had brought no coat or blanket to fend it off, but Joe acted like he did not even notice. He continued to push for every bit of speed he could get from the flagging animal.

As dawn was breaking behind him, Joe stopped to let the paint horse roll and briefly rest.

He himself found a spot out of the brisk wind that almost constantly blew up here. He stretched out in the warmth of the sunshine and caught a nap. He would need all the strength and stamina he could muster before this ride was done. Somewhere out on the plains far to the east, Ransom Holt was in a coach speeding to deliver Peabody's blood money.

Joe had to reach her first. He *had* to.

When he woke, he walked to the rim of the near vertical scarp that marked the eastern edge of South Park. He stood with eyes shaded, watching the shift of dark cloud shadow across the pale, rolling miles of grass that flourished on the floor of the vast bowl that was South Park. After a few minutes, he grunted softly to himself and nodded.

"There," he said aloud.

The paint's ears swiveled toward him and it raised its head, sprigs of sun-yellowed grass hanging out of its mouth.

"Good news for you, hoss," Joe said as he leaped again onto the paint's back. "There's a bunch o' mountain Utes over yonder. Might be I won't have to ride you t' death after all. Now come help me find my way down off this high rock. I know it can be done. I've done it before. So let's find the path and git along, shall we?"

✦ 60 ✦

"GREETINGS, BROTHER," JOE signed as he approached
the Ute camp. He rode into the middle of the camp
and dismounted without waiting for an invitation. "Spotted
Wolf, is that you? You are growing old and gray. Fat, too."
Spotted Wolf was as lean as his namesake.

The tall Indian grinned. "Old with wisdom, Man Killer."
He stepped forward and clasped Joe's hand. "Welcome, my
brother. Are you hungry? Do you thirst?"

It hadn't actually occurred to Joe, but . . . yes. Now that
he thought of it, he was famished. "I could eat a buffalo, I
think, and then I would ask when do we begin the meal."

Spotted Wolf and the other men of the band laughed,
and then he took Joe into his lodge, where the old warrior's
two young wives waited on them.

"Where is your old woman?" Joe asked. "The last time
I saw you . . ."

225

"Dead," Spotted Wolf said with a shrug. "These two"—the smile returned—"they are not dead, eh?" The gray-haired Ute cupped his crotch and chuckled.

"I am glad it is well with you, old friend." Joe started eating the rich stew served by Spotted Wolf's wives.

"And with you, Man Killer?"

Joe briefly explained the mission he was on.

"You would find this man and kill him?" Spotted Wolf said.

"He took what was mine," Joe said. "I will kill him or he will kill me. We shall see."

Spotted Wolf grunted his approval of Joe's intentions.

While his second bowl of stew was being prepared, Joe said, "My horse is a good one but he is tired and I have far to go. I would buy horses from you, friend."

"Buying horses, that is a serious thing. It needs much thought."

Dammit, Joe thought. Spotted Wolf had him over a barrel and intended to take advantage of him.

"I have no time, my brother, but I have much money to pay."

"Bah! Money. Why would I need money, Man Killer?" He held his hand palm up and indicated the earth around the place where they sat. "Will money buy this? No? Here is all a man could need."

"You see what I carry," Joe said. "No packs of goods this trip. Only money."

Spotted Wolf began loading tobacco into his pipe, suggesting they were about to begin serious negotiations. His eyes, Joe noticed, kept coming back to the Henry rifle that lay on the robes beside the place where Joe was sitting.

Probably there was not an Indian in these mountains who owned a repeating rifle. To have a Henry would give a man much prestige among his peers.

Blood at Bear Lake

An hour later, Joe was the owner of a string of five tough little Indian ponies. He could have gotten more for the Henry if he had been willing to haggle longer, but time was more important to him than any number of horses would have been.

"It is well," Joe said once they had shaken hands on the swap. "I will go now, brother."

"You will not stay? We would speak of the good times when we were young," Spotted Wolf said.

"I must go now. Catch this man who took what was mine. Perhaps I will come back by and by. We will sit by the fire, we two old warriors. Drink a little. Tell some lies. It will be good. Come now. I would choose my horses from your herd so that I can go and do what must be done." He stood and headed for the lodge entrance.

J OE RODE THROUGH the night, through the burning heat
of the following day, and far into the chill of night again.
Riding one horse and leading the others, he pushed each animal to exhaustion, then paused only long enough to change
the jaw rein to another horse and race on again.

By the time he approached Bear Lake, it was nearing
dawn and he was down to two horses, the others having been
worn out and abandoned to fend for themselves.

Joe was not sure where he might find Fiona, but he knew
where he could start looking. He headed for the trading
post run by an old friend.

Heedless of the hour, he slipped down off the delicate
gray he was on at the moment. His legs felt wobbly beneath
him after so long on horseback, but he forced them to carry
him to the door of the shack where Ezra did business.

Pounding on the door with his fist, Joe shouted, "Open
up in there, old man. You got company."

About the third or fourth time he pounded for entry, he heard a drowsy voice respond, "Open it yourself, y' damn fool. It ain't locked."

Feeling completely chagrined, he tried pulling the latch string. Sure as hell, the door opened easily.

When he stepped inside, he was immediately struck by the scent of tobacco, whale oil, and cinnamon. A small lamp with the wick trimmed low burned atop a counter. Behind the counter Joe could see two things, one being the bushy eyebrows and big nose of Ezra White, and the other being the muzzle of Ezra's old flintlock rifle.

"Ez, put that thing down before it blows up in your face an' makes you even uglier 'n you already are."

"Joe? Izzat you, Joe Moss? Well, I'll be a sonuvabitch." The rifle muzzle was quickly withdrawn behind the counter.

"Oh, hell, Ez, you already are that." Joe entered the crowded store, and Ezra turned his lamp up.

The old trapper was bedded down on a pallet behind his store counter. He had company, but Joe could not tell what tribe the young girl was from. She was naked. So, for that matter, was Ezra, but Joe had seen him bare-assed before.

"What're you here for, Joseph?"

"I'm lookin' for a man, Ez. I'm thinking you should know him."

"What's his name?"

"Charles."

"That his first name or his last?" Ezra glanced down at the naked teenager curled up at his side. He cuffed her on one ear and said, "Where's your manners? Git up an' brew us some coffee, woman."

The girl grabbed up her dress—Shoshone, Joe thought after getting a look at the sparse beadwork on her antelope-skin dress—and scurried off about her chores.

"Charles is all I was told," Joe said. "Could be either."

"There's a man . . . Jedediah Charles . . . has a shack a couple miles from here. If you don't mind me askin', Joseph, does this here have anything to do with the heap o' cash money Jedediah says he's expectin' to get any day now?"

Joe nodded, his expression grim. "It do."

Ez cocked an eye at Joe for a moment, then asked, "Mind telling me are you here to deliver that money?"

"That ain't what I'm wanting of him, Ez. He has something that's mine. I figure to take it back."

Ezra grunted, then asked, "Need any help?"

"No, but I thank you for askin'."

Ezra grunted again, louder this time, then stood and reached for his britches. "Come over here. I'll show you how to find him."

Joe felt a tightening in his throat as he hurried to Ezra's counter. Close. He was so very close to Fiona now.

✛ 62 ✛

THE PLACE WAS a dugout, a man-made cave dug into a hillside and roofed over with aspen poles and sod. Logs had been laid up to form the front wall, then chinked with mud.

A pole corral nearby held three horses and a pair of burros. One of those horses Joe knew well. It was Fiona's swift and leggy little sorrel mare, the horse she had been riding the last time he saw her.

The horse had not been swift enough to keep her from harm this time, though. If he had only been with her . . .

Joe forced all unproductive fantasy out of mind. Now was what counted, not what might have been.

He rode up to the corral, slipped to the ground, and tied his horses to the top rail. "Hello the house," he called loud and firm. "Is Jedediah Charles here?"

The elk hide that served as a door was pushed aside and a large, bearded man stepped out.

"You're Charles?"

"I am. Now who would you be?"

"I'm the man as come to inspect Ransom Holt's merchandise. I believe you have some for him."

"What? He don't trust us?"

"Us," Charles had said. That implied he had a partner, probably inside where he could get to Fiona and harm her if things went wrong. Joe needed everyone to be out here where he could see them.

He asked the question he most dreaded to have answered. "Is the woman alive?"

"Holt said we could do what we wanted with her," Charles whined. "I got to tell you, though, she ain't all that good a fuck. Won't wiggle an' give a man his satisfaction like a Injun girl will." He smiled. "But you can tell Mr. Holt we done what he said. Got a nice little cask over there just the right size to put her head in an' the pickling salts to go in with it. Everything just like he wanted."

Salts and a keg. Jesus God!

But Joe was careful to keep the loathing that he felt out of his face. "Bring her out so I can get a look at her an' make sure you got the right one. Mr. Holt won't pay for just any woman, you know."

"Oh, we got the right one, all right." Charles snorted. "Bitch keeps telling us her man Joe Moss is gonna skin us alive an' nail our hides to that wall to dry. It's her, all right."

Joe nodded and made a vow that he intended to keep over the coming hours. If Fiona wanted these two skinned alive, then so be it. That was a job that would give Joe no grief. And it occurred to him that a keg intended for Fiona's dear head could just as easily hold Ransom Holt's pickled head. Pack it and ship it to Peabody. Freight collect! That ought to get the bastard's attention.

"Drag her out here then so's I can see," Joe said.

Charles raised his voice. "Vincent. Bring her out so the gentleman can get a look at her." To Joe, he said, "Will you know her when you see her?"

Joe's hands were trembling and his breath was short and shallow. He hoped Charles could not see that. "I'll know if it's her," he said.

The elk hide was pulled back, and Joe could hear chains rattle. A moment more, and a filthy, naked human form was dragged into the open by the seller's partner. Joe had eyes only for the captive.

She was skinny, wasted away to skin and bone. But that shock of flaming red hair was undimmed and so was her spirit.

Believing the man had come who would behead her, she refused to give him the satisfaction of so much as glancing in his direction or in any way acknowledging his existence.

Joe's heart skipped a beat. Probably several.

Fiona. His own Fiona.

She was chained hand and foot. Joe scowled and said, "You got the keys to those padlocks?"

"Right here." Charles held a key ring aloft.

Joe grunted, then took his tomahawk out of his sash.

He very carefully and judiciously smashed Jedediah Charles over the head with it, then laid into the man's partner as well. These two he wanted to take down alive. He wanted them alive and screaming when he and Fiona commenced flaying them. Exactly like she said would be done. Skin the bastards and nail their hides up to dry. It would give him and Fiona something to do while they waited for Holt to arrive with Charles's stinking blood money.

Ah, but Ransom Holt. Joe turned his head and spat. That son of a bitch belonged to Joe. And Joe wanted Holt alive when Joe took first his scalp and then his head.

For now, though . . .

Joe lifted Fiona into his arms and began the slow but satisfying process of kissing away the terrors she had undergone since he last saw her.

Now if they could only find and reclaim their sweet daughter, Jessica, all would soon be well.